THE DEVICE
THE DEVIL
& ME

STEPHANIE TAYLOR

The Linen Press

For Anouska, my beautiful sister
And for my Mum
For ever

Published in the UK by
The Linen Press
75c(13) South Oswald Rd
EDINBURGH
EH9 2HH
www.linenpressbooks.co.uk

First published by The Linen Press, August 2009

Copyright © Stephanie Taylor, 2009

All rights reserved. This book is sold subject to the condition
that it shall not, by way of trade or otherwise, be lent, re-sold,
hired out or otherwise circulated in any form or by any means, electronic,
mechanical, photocopying, recording or otherwise
without prior written permission

ISBN 978-0-95596-184-7

Typeset and designed by Initial Typesetting Services, Edinburgh
Printed and bound by M&A Thomson Litho Ltd

Acknowledgements

I would first of all like to thank Lynn Michell who has nurtured this book from its very beginning when I wandered into her writing group, the Monday Lovelies, full of ideas and emotions. Her help, encouragement, wisdom and belief have given me the strength to see this project through to the book you hold. Thank you, thank you!

A big thank you goes to Debbie Miller, whose glowing critique made me believe in my writing and write what is in my heart. Thanks must also go to my friends at the Tyne and Esk Writers' groups, especially the Penicuik crew and David C. Purdie, who listens tirelessly every fortnight to new work and ideas.

I am the luckiest girl in the world because of my friends and family. I would like to thank you all for your love and support through everything, not just the writing of this book. To those of you who have read the manuscript in various drafts and kept encouraging me I would like to give a special mention; Natalie, Rachel, Alice and my fantastic gran who has the best comedy timing in the land – but doesn't even know it!

And to Bea, who knows I will always be her number one fan. I love you all so much.

And finally, I don't know why I write, but I know why I live: my boys. Julian, Sonny and Cohen, with all my love, I thank you x x

Lucky Girl

So I'm sitting here in a bit of a pickle.

Possibly the worst one yet.

I look over at the bits and bobs lying on the table: fingertips, toes, a wrist with a bracelet around it.

I am trying to figure out which part of my body I inhabit. I know this is a self-destructive process; if I find what I am looking for I will have already lost it, but I can't help it.

I started with the easy bits.

About an hour ago I cut off my hair. No change, except I began to realise I'd only grown it because I thought it might make me look sexy.

Then fingernails. Obviously no change. I remembered how long it took me to stop biting them to the quick until the tips were numb and gloves were painful to wear.

The fingers were harder. I started with a pinkie: Yakuza style.

As I now progress further through the digits and limbs I don't feel any different but every lost part of my body has a memory attached to it.

Maybe I need to find the story that connects the pieces. What is it? How far can I take this? I'm not a silly girl. I know how this will end if I carry on, but I just can't stop.

Maybe I exist in compulsion.

I do, however, begin to feel reluctant as I reach my thighs.

I start to lament their loss and worry that I might be taking things a bit too far.

I think about what will happen when I cut off my lips, my smile. I know I couldn't exist without a smile. Could I?

And then it happens. My ears detect the faint yet unmistakable sound of music seeping through the walls, the fabulous opening bars...

'First I was afraid, I was petrified.'

My senses prick and I see my toes twitching on the table.

'Kept thinking I could never live without you by my side.'

My excitement bubbles as I can feel movement begin to overtake me. My dismembered cells start pulling together and pulse to the tonic only Gloria Gaynor can provide. All the fragments of myself gather and reattach themselves to the core I haven't yet dissected.

The music gets louder.

'But I spent so many nights, thinking how you did me wrong.'

As if a switch is flicked on I start jumping and smiling. I strut around my room with my heartbeat banging through my veins. The jewelled feather tiara and sequined dress I have magically donned (and secretly always wear) glimmer and sparkle.

'I grew strong.'

At this moment I am conscious of a union between me and my body.

'And I learned how to get along.'

We are am.

I am we.

I am them and they are me.
I know where I exist!
I am a lucky girl.
I can dance.

I have a secret

I am mad.

Not crazy or bonkers or daft.

Just mad.

You wouldn't know it to look at me or talk to me or even be in a loving long-term relationship with me, but I can assure you, I have the darkness.

I have disguised my madness so well that I cannot now reveal it.

I lead two lives. This one where I interact normally with people, and the real one where I exist in my own head.

Sometimes I like it.

Sometimes I revel in it because it makes me feel special.

But mostly I want it to go.

Then I worry that if it goes, do I go too?

Is there a payoff?

If I am no longer mad, will I still be able to paint and write and dance and oh no...

What if I never laugh again?

The risk is too great.

For now I will remain.

Me.

Where to Start?

Where shall I start my story?
   What would you like to hear?
   What would I like you to hear?
   All I know is that I have always felt a little out of place – a little skew-wiff if you like. I don't usually tell people my secrets but sometimes I feel like I might burst with the pressure of keeping it all in. I know I'm bad but I don't feel like a bad person. I hope I can show you this.
   I hope
   You
   Will
   Like
   me.

The Devil

You see, you're safe from God and Jesus and the like.

You're safe because you have to ask them in. You have to actively seek them out. You can of course live in awe of their creation and walk around in a daze of amazement at the beautiful world but if you want to be part of the gang you have to ask. You are always invited, that is an absolute. There is always space for you at the party, but you have to RSVP.

The thing is the Devil doesn't need a reply. The Devil will have you at his party whether you want to go or not. He will lay traps and temptations. You may not know about any of this, and to be honest, I feel bad about telling you because now you know, you will always know. Just like me.

And if you know, you must fight.

My problem is this: I don't want the Devil but I don't want Jesus either.

Can you have one without the other?

At church I never felt the love of the Holy Spirit, only the terror.

The Sure Thing

I can't remember a time when he wasn't there. My strange companion. The girls in my class at primary school talked about imaginary friends and how they played and got into mischief, but my companion was different. He wasn't someone I conjured up for play. I spent the whole time hiding from him, not wanting a soul to find out. Once, I tried to give life to a little square of air by my feet like the other girls but it felt fake. I visualised a character; he was a little ball of fluff with legs that I called Anthony Pants. When my friends weren't looking, I would kick him over the fence out of the playground into the wild bit.

Anthony Pants wasn't ever real. I knew that and it scared me.

It scared me because it meant that the presence that came to me in the night in invisible waves *was* real.

The first time I felt His presence was when I was two or three. My Mum and Dad and I had moved to a new house in the country. That first night, I lay in my bed staring at the wall. The patterns on the unfamiliar wallpaper started to shift and move. They became sticks and bones and skeletons fighting and stabbing at one another. Even when I shut my eyes the battles continued and intensified. I tried to call to my Mum but no sound came out of my mouth. I could hear muffled voices in the next room. The air around me felt close and electric. The voices grew louder and more angry making my head prickle deep inside. I folded my ears into themselves to block out the noise and squeezed my eyelids together to shut out the frantic wallpaper.

In the morning I woke up cold and wet and shivering.

My Mum looked cross and tired as she bundled my sheets into the washing machine and scrubbed my mattress with Dettol.

'It's all right darling.' She cuddled me into her when she was finished. 'You'll get used to this new house soon.'

In the daytime I believed her and felt happy.

Sleep

I wish the sleep would just come.

I wish I could freefall into it without a care... but the Demons try to grab me as I slip down,

down,

down...

There, nearly there, damn it. That realisation is a curse. A curse. A glimpse of clarity at completely the wrong moment.

Try again.

I lie still and relaxed and yet my guards stay firmly up. I sink into the pillow deeper and deeper. It grips my head harder and harder.

Shit, I forgot to pray.

Now I am awake, again. I will have to rebuild my guards piece by piece but only after my prayer.

How did I forget to pray?

Every night for as long as I can remember, I have prayed for world peace.

It is the same prayer night after night, only now at least I don't have to repeat it twice to make sure it will work. It took a long time to grasp that inconsistencies in my rituals do not really seem to make that much difference to anything, let alone world peace.

My prayers, although consistent, are not altogether altruistic. I think that they veer towards spiritual insurance. Although the idea shames me, I can't help feeling that maybe that is the point of religion.

I could have told you that every night I pray for world peace and left it at that. But no, I have to make sure that you know there are negative angles and that praying doesn't make me a good person.

In fact my prayer is more like a mantra. I know it more by its rhythm than its words. When I recite it, it undulates in a cosy hole in the top right part of my brain. Its movements are so familiar to me that I can engage my brain in other activities around it. I can plan my next day, or think of a story. Anything. This used to upset me immensely. If I distracted myself at all I would have to return to the beginning and start again. But so great is my capacity for distraction that I would have to start four or five times in a row. This coupled with the fact that I had to repeat it twice anyway could make praying a bit of an ordeal. Especially since I am only guessing at the consequences of uncorrected mistakes.

Right, I am straying. Start again.

'This night as I lay down to sleep...' I'm feeling embarrassed about my prayer. It's like sharing the most intimate part of myself with you. I don't want to tell you this bit first but it is at the start so I have to.

'I pray the lord my soul to keep...' I think of this as the first section. Like a straight line.

'If I die before I wake, I pray the lord my soul to take...' There. I got through the whole beginning without getting it mixed up and praying for the lord to take my soul before saying 'If I die...' as this would mean praying for my own death which would mean the Devil would get me.

Now the peace bit.

'God bless everybody and everything. And please help everybody and everything find peace in their hearts and spread it throughout

the world. Amen.' I see this as a vast wave engulfing everything in its path. Like the shockwave after a huge blast. The wave is love that soothes and pacifies as it breaks over the world.

The fact that I can break my prayer up and simultaneously give you a running commentary shows me how much it has become devalued in my own head. I don't think I believe it any more.

I could try not saying it one night.

I think I might go to the doctor

Sometimes I wondered how it was possible that everyone seemed to have no idea about the real me. I shook if a gypsy or fortune teller came into the shop. I made an excuse and darted through to the stockroom, half expecting to be followed by sharp pointing fingers and I always expected an interrogation after dinner.

Maybe not.

Maybe I was a master of disguise.

Maybe my confident, smiling alter ego had everyone fooled.

Nevertheless, I thought I should go to the doctor.

But more than that, I just wanted to tell someone, to release myself from my burden. If I started with a stranger maybe it would be easier.

I wanted to tell my Mum.

I couldn't possibly tell my Mum.

I wanted to tell Nick.

I couldn't possibly tell Nick.

I made the appointment. 11 a.m. Tuesday. I didn't tell anyone. Luckily it was my day off.

While I was sitting in the waiting room I thought up things to tell the doctor: cystitis? I was prone to that. Migraine? I was prone to that too. Insomnia? Not valid, I battled but always got there in the end.

By the time my name was buzzed through the jarring intercom

I had decided upon cystitis. I took my seat opposite the doctor. She had a serious face but a plump friendly body and before I could stop myself, I told her.

I told her everything.

'I hurt myself,' I said.

I cried.

'I make myself sick,' I said.

I cried more and she handed me a box of tissues with the top tissue perfectly poised for the plucking. I reached over and plucked it. I was reminded of grieving widows with petticoats, flicking their handkerchiefs with a flourish and dabbing their noses. I didn't dab. I soaked the soft paper to a salty pulp and reached for another.

'Have you told anyone?' Her arm was still extended with the box attached.

'No, you're the first.' I sniffed. 'I want to tell my Mum but she'd be so disappointed.'

The doctor gave me a form with twenty questions that I had to answer by placing a cross on a grading line. Further to the left was 'not at all'; further to the right was 'all of the time'.

I don't remember what the questions were, only that the answer sheet had crosses all down the right of it. When I had finished, I was worried I had just been exaggerating for effect. Perhaps I had wanted to impress the doctor. I immediately felt like a fraud.

'What if I'm lying?'

'Are you lying?'

'I don't know.' My head was on my knees throbbing with confusion. What if I *was* lying? I felt okay most of the time, but a separate part of me kept shouting out, an irrational part that couldn't keep secrets. I was doing okay before this helpless little corner got bigger and edged its way in. It jutted and poked at me, making me question my actions.

'I'm fine really, I run a successful shop, I have a wonderful boyfriend, my family love me. I have no idea why I came today. Can we just forget about it please? I feel so silly.' I looked at her with eyes that must have been bloodshot. 'Please help me,' I said. 'I want this to stop.'

The doctor's stare held me in its grip.

'You have been very brave coming today and telling me this.' Relief. I was brave. The doctor began to type things into her computer. 'I am going to write you a referral, Lauren,' she said, looking at me yet still typing. It reminded me of my Mum. 'I think you have dealt with this on your own for far too long.'

'Thank you.' It was all I could say.

'In the meantime, we should discuss medication.'

'No.'

'Are you sure, Lauren?'

'It's not chemical.' I said. 'I know it's not.'

She smiled.

On the way home in the bus I kept thinking about my Great-Granny's crochet blanket. It was a multicoloured chain stitch cover with many brothers and sisters. I think my Great-Granny must have made hundreds in her lifetime. They were used for everything from throws for sofas and beds, shoulder warmers for giving orphan lambs their night bottle, shrouds for long loved pets, hangover comforters. All through my life, if I was chilly or ill, I would reach for one of my Great-Granny's blankets.

In the bus that took for ever to creep down Leith walk, I craved one of the blankets to wrap around my back and shoulders. The longing became an ache; I needed to be held in the familiar colours and holey stitching.

When I got home my blanket was waiting for me on the sofa. I leapt onto it, curled my toes under my body and pulled the corners of the cover around me. It was brown and orange and cream and pink and black. It really wasn't one of her best. I don't think colour composition was ever a factor; more what wool was to hand. I took extra comfort in the image of my wizened Granny on a wardrobe-raiding frenzy in search of jumpers to un-pick and rip down.

I rested my chin on my shoulder rubbing it against the blanket and smiled. It wasn't even that cosy with its big loose stitches. I self-consciously smiled again.

Brave.

That's what the doctor had said. I was brave. I felt like a little girl with a rosette at a gymkhana.

Deep in the smallest darkest bit of myself, I felt battle commence. I knew the time was right.

Nick

I have lived with Nick for two years but we have been together for ever. We met when I was sixteen and he was an impossibly swoonsome mature eighteen.

It was on a night out with my best friend Kitty when I first caught sight of Nick. It was a Friday night and we were at the cool part of town where people wore black clothes and army store boots.

It was perfect for me.

Kitty knew about these places because in second year at our local high school her Mum and Dad thought it would be a good idea to accelerate her learning by putting her into one of Edinburgh's many private schools. So far, her parents' investment had taught her how to roll a joint, where all the cool people hung out and that if you stuck to vodka you wouldn't get a hangover.

We walked into the beer garden of the Pear Tree trying not to look underage. The trick was to be very serious. If you appeared humourless you looked absolutely like a grown up.

Kitty waved to a group of scruffy-looking, gangly kids a few tables away. As we walked over my heart started to rattle on the inside of my chest. One of the gangly kids was not gangly or a kid at all. He was simply gorgeous.

'Who's that?' I asked Kitty on the way to the bar. She rolled her eyes.

'I *knew* you'd fancy him.' She cuddled into my arm. 'That's Nick.'

'He's gorgeous.' I felt shy. 'Has he got a girlfriend?'

'Na, don't think he's interested in girls much. Too cool or something.'

We rejoined the group with our drinks. By the end of the night Nick and I were kissing and I had his phone number written in my eyeliner on a Rizla paper.

He had kept me enthralled all evening with his smoky eyes and River Phoenix hair while he taught me things about the world.

He didn't drink Coca-cola; he hated multi-nationals. I nodded in agreement, sucking on my vodka, thanking the lord I had chosen to mix it with tonic.

He would dismiss any one who started to tell a racist or sexist joke. He was a revelation in manhood.

I was in love.

So now we have been together for nearly eight years and I still tremble when I see him walking towards me.

He is the quiet constant in my life and I endeavour to show him only my best side.

I look at the fridge

I look at the fridge.
 Don't look.
 I stare through the TV and smoke.
 I glance at the cupboard.
 Don't glance.
 I stare back through the TV and smoke. My eyes go to the cupboard again and my body follows. I will just have a small sandwich. Bread, no butter. Thin, thin cheese and pickle, I don't want to undo the good at the gym this morning, but everybody eats dinner, don't they? That can't hurt. The body needs fuel. I pop a slice of cheese into my mouth before I finish making the sandwich and have to cut another to replace it. By the time I sit down with the plate on my knee I've made the decision. Just once more then I promise I will be done with this filth. I squeeze the rest of the sandwich into my mouth and wash it down with some Diet Coke. I go to make another. Toasted thick bread this time with lashings of butter. I'm not shy about slicing the cheese either, one for me, one for my sandwich. I add mayo, pickle, tomatoes and mashed potato.
 The guilt starts but there's no going back now. I need to sate this urge.

The Truth

I crouched in my familiar position, at once comforting and shameful, over the toilet. I looked into the clear water in the bleached bowl.

Usually this was something I did mechanically, without thinking. But this time was different.

An old relative had just died. I could feel his dead eyes all around me, watching. Disappointed, ashamed, angry. As soon as this image entered my head, the eyes turned into those of my Granddad, then my Great Gran's, until I was surrounded by the eyes and judgement of all the dead I had known. Then all the dead I hadn't known joined in. I was crushed with shame and humiliation but I felt the fat forming on my upper arms.

I took a breath, with them all watching and paused... and started to think about a childhood friend of mine called Lucy.

I knew I was different from Lucy the first time I met her. I was only a year older. She was two, I was three. I was bigger and taller, which was normal, but I grew a lot bigger and a lot taller. She stayed slight. She was the kind of girl who could be given sweeties and chocolate and save them for later, producing them triumphantly after yours were finished.

Lucy would eat Wotsits by biting each crisp in half, eating one side and returning the remaining piece to the packet until only the halves were left. These too would be left until later. These were some of the little differences between us.

The main difference though, even then, was that she was skinny. I deduced at a very young age therefore, that I must be fat, a feeling that sprained through me and filled me with anxiety. I felt hefty and ungainly. My awkwardness prevented me from playing childhood games with complete abandon. Despite this, my Mum took me along to a gymnastics class. It turned out I had natural ability as my joints were hyper-mobile. I could do splits and walkovers with ease and, at last, felt proud of myself.

Lucy didn't go to gymnastics so I took a certain satisfaction from teaching her, aware that she was not as limber as I was. We would spend hours in the garden making up routines and practising moves.

One glorious day, one of the frequently delivered bin-bags of hand-me-down clothes arrived from my cousins. While raking through the jeans and t-shirts I came across two sequin-clad leotards. I was ecstatic about this unexpected treasure. I felt Olympic as Lucy and I went over our routines in sequins wishing and imagining we had real asymmetric bars to match our leotards not just the bending crossbars of Lucy's swing. Round and round we somersaulted until at last my Dad came home from work.

An Audience!

'Watch this! Watch this!'

We ran up to him excited and proud to show him what we'd made up. I began the routine by walking to him, chin up, toes pointed, showing off my new turquoise leotard.

'Oh!' he said, looking at me with a smile on his face. 'Look at your wee pot belly!'

I quickly pulled in my tummy and did my routine with humiliation stinging my face.

I didn't wait for the applause. I ran to the bathroom.

I remembered all this with my elbows pressing on the toilet seat and the dead eyes staring down on me. I hadn't thought of that for years. With the ghosts and memories crowding my actions, I took another deep breath and went on and did what I had intended to.

Devil 2

I have a tan.

Therefore I have freckles.

Therefore the sign will be beginning to appear on my forehead. Freckles will be joining up to spell 666. I daren't even check in the mirror. I wear my cap or pull my fringe over my face at all times.

I should check in the mirror.

I stand before it, eyes down.

I raise my face, eyes tight shut.

I open my eyes.

Dark shadows swarm and writhe around me. I flee. I flee so quickly that I don't have a chance to check my forehead.

Freedom

'Oh shit.'

The cubicle door opened and Kitty's face peered out, pale.

'You'll never guess what I've just done.'

'You've dropped it down the toilet,' I joked, waiting to be ushered into the loo beside her.

'Worse.' Her face showed no sign of humour.

I pushed past her and looked at the dirty wet floor and sure enough, there was a drain and through the dark filthy grating was a little pill.

'Oh shit.' We looked at each other.

'No, that's really shit.' Kitty looked worried as if I were going to give her a row. I pulled her towards me and we giggled into each other's night out costumes. We had managed to get hold of a solitary pill in our favourite jungle club and had planned on sharing it in the safety of the ladies.

Drugs.

They were great, for as long as they kept you high, they kept Him at bay. Completely. He disappeared without a trace. For a small time I could be me. Alcohol did the same.

'Do you think we can get it out?' I said, optimistically, knowing the truth. We could see it dissolving before our eyes.

There's nothing like losing drugs to spoil a night. Reluctantly and slowly we checked ourselves in the mirrors. My reflection was good. I looked good. I was pleased. In fact I was elated despite the loss of our pill. I could hear the thump of the bass through the walls and it hit me in the throat. I could feel myself starting to move and I took Kitty by the arm.

'Come on, it's our tune!' Panic rising in case we missed the track we came for, we bounced out of the toilets and made our way through the darkly dressed people in the darkly lit club to dance to the ultra dark music. It was so low and dark, you could hear it with your body.

The heavy beats and squelchy noises vibrated through me and lifted me high from the chest upwards. It was an amazing feeling and I held my hands up in the air – moving, jumping, smiling towards the speakers and DJ box.

Kitty and I turned our faces towards each other at the same time. Her face matched my feelings perfectly: all smiling teeth and eyes. We held on to each other's shoulders as we bounced. The place was packed and the heat and moisture from the other bodies was exhilarating. Everyone I looked at was smiling.

Everyone was happy.

'This is fucking amazing, Laur. We've gotta get more drugs!'

We wanted to get higher higher higher.

My heart was racing.

I kept dancing and moving. I felt so free.

After about ten unmissable tracks we took a break and sat down on the floor in the hallway.

'You on owt?' A skeletal regular stared into our faces through moon eyes.

'Na, clever baws here dropped our stash down the bog.'

'That's tough man, here, take these. They're 2CBs, like a mix ay eccies and acid and they've no been classified yet so they're no even illegal.'

'Any good?'

'Fuckin' barry, man!' He gave us one each and we took it. Just like that.

*

It was later in bed when the creeping set in.

Why did I do it?

Why?

When I knew what the consequences were every time.

To be without the Devil for any length of time meant payback.

Now I was paying.

Sleep eluded me. I chanted. I visualised. I prayed. But every time I was about to fall into sweet slumber He gently but firmly tapped me on the shoulder, reminding me how bad I was.

> *The consequence.*
> *You'll die, you idiot.*
> *You idiot.*
> *Fancy taking a pill from a stranger and dying.*
> *What a fucking idiot.*
> *Only the lowest of the low die from drugs and you know what? They slip so sweetly into my arms.*
> *I'm waiting...*
> *Remember that.*

I was so scared I clutched my duvet with hands and teeth.
 I didn't want to die.
 I didn't want to die so I had to wait.

> *I lay out my tools before me.*
> *One device.*
> *One lead box, head size.*
> *One clear tarpaulin bag.*
> *One delicious blade.*
> *Everything is ready.*

Body

I don't know why but something makes me look under the bed.

A transparent tarpaulin clings to the form of a human body with blood and fluids pooling on its inner surface. I feel myself turn cold and my stomach curls into a knot. I shakily get out of bed and suck in some deep breaths. I make it on to my bare feet. They squirm against the carpet as I creep through to the living room where Nick is watching telly.

'Sweetheart, I've just had the most awful dream.' My heart is still racing.

'What was it?' He pats the sofa and I go to sit by him.

'There was a body under the bed and it was me who killed it.' Nick looks at me with the strangest mixture of fear and confusion. He sometimes gets more distressed by my nightmares than I do. I wait for his words of comfort so I can go back to sleep.

'Darling,' he says with his head cocked as if to explain something I should already know. 'That wasn't a dream.'

Larder Than Life

I worked in a secondhand book shop. It was owned by a charming old gent called Charles who pretty much left me to get on with things by myself, only popping in once a fortnight for a coffee and a chat under the guise of checking up on the business. I had worked there for about five years and found it comforting.

I was left to my own devices as usual and it was a slow dull day. There were jobs that needed doing but I couldn't seem to summon the enthusiasm. After a couple of bored, boring hours I finally left my position behind the counter and went over to the shelf that needed rearranging. I hoped it would keep my mind off myself and how I looked for a while.

I was getting fixated and I knew it.

On the way to the shelf I tried not to look in the mirror.

I turned my head. Damn it.

I looked.

I saw.

I was hideous. Fat. Ugly. It wasn't enough that I went swimming every morning and training every evening. I still indulged in too much food and as I stared in the mirror turning this way and that, I felt my self-loathing reach deeper in to me.

It was during this moment of self scrutiny that my Mum popped into the shop and I noticed that she was getting fatter.

Not only was I forever criticising my own appearance, I scrutinised every person I met. I knew the exact proportion of the perfect wrist, perfect bum, perfect breasts, perfect ankles.

I didn't have any of them – except my neck. If I stopped giving myself a hard time for being conceited for a minute, I could admit that I had a good neck. Long and feminine. It was the perfect neck, and, when I allowed it to, it gave me hope.

No one was immune from my critique but when it was my Mum who caught my eye for slipping, I felt uncomfortable and nauseous.

From when I was very small, my mother taught me to walk tall with my shoulders back, tummy tucked in, and she told me about my pelvic floor. 'You know, women just seem to let themselves go after they have children. There's no need for it. It's sheer laziness,' she would tell me while doing sit-ups with her feet tucked under the sofa, exposing her perfectly formed freckled ankles. I would look at my chunky tree stumps in dismay. When I was about fourteen, my Mum had taken me out to a posh Edinburgh hair salon. It was a swanky establishment and I felt very grown up in the efficient sparkling surroundings. I rested my feet on the foot bar under the mirror. I was wearing slip on shoes with no socks. I was feeling elegant with my choice of apparel until I looked down to admire my new shoes: a pair I felt sure would get equal attention at school on Monday.

What I saw changed me.

The sight was horrible. The ends of my legs joined my feet with a chubby band like a baby's. They weren't elegant at all.

They weren't even normal. I'd never seen anything like them before. I looked around at the tiny creatures dressed in black, scissors in hand, padding about on perfectly sculpted little legs and I became obsessed about ankle bones from that day.

On that day my ankles were thick and swollen and on this day in the shop that's how my Mum looked. Her body was thick and swollen. Everything was turgid. Her fingers were hard, her neck was thick and her face was puffed.

I was ashamed of my disgust.

I felt shallow but I found it difficult to talk to her.

She had let herself go.

'I'm really breathless,' she told me. Her breath smelled funny: sweet and sour and not from her mouth but from deep in her belly. I had to look away because the words, 'it's 'cos you're so fat' were bouncing around my brain. I was worried she might ask me about her appearance.

'Do I look okay? Is my hair all right?' Thankfully she focused on her hair which always looked fabulous.

'Yes, Mum. It's perfect.' I turned away. She didn't ask about the rest of her and for that I was grateful.

> *The origin.*
>
> *So where do you come from?*
>
> *Don't ask Him, stop questioning – it leaves holes for entry.*
>
> *He might answer.*
>
> *I know where anyway. He comes in through the tiny dot of white light that remains in the middle of the screen when you switch off the telly. Just as you hear that bit of static – that's where.*
>
> *He creeps up behind you as you're about to look in the mirror.*

He comes out of the mouths of people who speak about evil things and dives straight into yours – That's why you leave immediately when the people mention Ouija boards or tarot cards or hypnosis or war or nuclear power or Chernobyl or Hiroshima or fire or ice age or Jesus or God or Him.

He scales through the top of your head if you forget to construct your box around it before you go to sleep.

But most of all he gets in if you don't stick to the rules.

Just a flash

I decided to tell my Granny June about my nightmares.

I really loved my Granny June. She was a capable, strict old woman whose manner was often sarcastic and her humour black. She had no time for illness or weak behaviour in anyone else but she doted on my every whim. When I was a wee girl, she would indulge me with cakes and sweets and TV and wink conspiratorially when my Mum came to pick me up after a visit.

When my sister and I were little, Granny June would take us out for ice cream. We would sit in the car looking out over the harbour eating our treats. My sister and I with chocolate cones, Granny June with a strawberry and vanilla wafer. I was never brave enough to waste my one ice cream on anything other than chocolate. Well, I did once try a strawberry cone but couldn't enjoy it for thinking about chocolate. How could anyone not get chocolate? We would stare out at the windsurfers and I would recount the adventures of my dreams in great never-ending monologues.

'Oh for goodness sake, Lauren,' Granny June would say, 'I don't know where you get all this from. A dream is just a flash. An image. Not some big drawn out story.' So I would keep her amazed with my visual feasts pulling out every detail to impress her – colours, dialogue, storylines. I didn't always know whether they were dreamt or made up at that moment.

So there I was sitting with Granny June. She had shortened the light cable. She had moaned for two days about its being too long and who was going to help her, what with no capable men in the family. Not that she would ask them even if there were. I said I'd do it the next time I came round to see her. But there I was and it had already been done. She had got the ladders in and had done it herself. Painted the ceiling while she was at it – not that she ever has any visitors to see her ceiling.

We were eating ham sandwiches – the kind from the tin, all jelly and grind. I'd already managed to sneak one up my sleeve to the bathroom and flushed it away, a trick my sister and I had perfected through years of corned beef and Spam. A tip for floating foodstuffs: place loads of toilet paper over the item before you flush, and behold, a clear bowl.

I hadn't told June about my dreams for years. Certainly not since they had started getting more sinister. When she ate, she spoke with her mouth open, full of white bread, saliva and clacking teeth. I felt ready to tell her.

'I had a horrible dream last night, Gran...'

Immediately she spoke.

'Oh *I* had the weirdest dream. I'd lost my handbag – a red handbag – I think it was my mother's or maybe it was yours. I was raking and raking all night in the wardrobe looking for it. What do you think that means?' She leant back in her chair triumphant.

We sat in silence.

I waited for a bit to see if she remembered that I was telling her about my dream.

She didn't. I was glad.

Highs and Flows

High blood pressure, that's what it was.

She'd been at an appointment with the practice nurse for her new patient registration and had been informed while the pressure band was still inflated, 'You shouldn't even be standing, Ms Swan!'

'You know, I have been seeing black spots and sparkles recently and my eyesight is atrocious.' My Mum was recanting the tale over herbal tea on an afternoon shopping trip.

'Why didn't you tell us, Mum? It's serious you know!'

'Oh it wasn't that bad. I was more worried about my weight being so gross.' She hadn't mentioned this before but her admission had showed how it had been playing on her mind. 'Turns out my thyroid's underactive too so I'm on thyroxin.'

I was ashamed of my secret joy – how wonderful for there to be a medical reason for my Mum's weight gain, leaving her integrity and beauty intact in my mind. Once the drugs kicked in, I was sure she'd be back to normal in a few weeks.

I didn't concern myself with why she might have developed these conditions and neither, it seemed, did anyone else. We finished our tea break and, satisfied, continued shopping.

> *I feel his hand on my shoulder.*
> *I am terrified.*
> *It is not a physical hand but the Devil's hand reminding me he is there. Always there.*

I am sitting in the church.

I have set up all my barriers tight around my head. I feel the demons; they are being deflected. So far. All the people around me shine with the glory of Christ. Surely they must see? I listen to them speaking in tongues. A chink appears in my armour and a tiny piece of my soul slips through on to the road to Hell. I patch up the hole quickly and begin my silent anti-evil mantra.

'Not here, not now, get away get away. Not here, not now, get away get away...'

Oh God, the pastor is looking at me. The world slows. They are handing out Bibles. I turn my face and with all my courage I look at one. Miraculously, it doesn't burst into flames. The evil in me must be conducted only through touch. I could be sick with relief. Maybe He is playing a trick on me. Maybe I have been sent to this place of worship to spy. The Devil is watching through my eyes and stealing their praise.

It will only make him stronger.

The friendly doctor who used his first name

I didn't know where to start.

I had only waited a few weeks for this referral. Now I wasn't sure if I was worthy of this attention.

What to say.

What the hell was I doing here?

He just watched me expectantly. Expecting what? What did he want? What did he want me to say?

I had two overwhelming images ramming my mind. I wanted to tell but I felt stupid.

'I don't know what to talk about.' I was wringing my hands over and over again. I pulled a tissue out of the box and picked off little bits and rolled them into tiny hard cigarettes and piled them up on the chair arm. If I dropped them all, I wondered, would they be hoovered up by next week? I lifted my head slightly and caught his eye.

Damn it.

He had introduced himself as Graham. I would have rather it had been Dr Hill like the sign on the door had said.

'What are you expecting from these sessions?'

I don't fucking know, you fucker. I want you to fix me. Don't make me tell you. I want fixed!

I felt like if I said *fix me* he'd just ask what needed fixed and I didn't know what was wrong. I wanted him to tell me. I wanted a pigeon-hole, but I was too embarrassed to ask for one.

Show me some fucking inkblots. I'd be good at that.

'I have images.'

'Do you have any now?'

'Two...'

I paused and took a huge breath, I felt as if all the exhaustion in the world had come and whipped out the last of my energy.

'I want to either lie at your feet and sleep on that carpet for a month or a year. Or...' I looked down at my hand. 'I want to lay my arm on this armrest then stab a big knife right through it to the wood and leave it there.' I made the chopping action with my right hand and wished it really had the blade in it.

'Which one would you prefer?'

'To sleep of course,' I said to him but I kept the truth to myself.

Love Is...

How odd it should look like half a love heart.
Just half.
It was Him; He put it there when I brushed too near a nail in the stockroom.
It had scratched and was sore but I didn't realise He had done it.
Half a love heart.
Only half.
Such an invitation to complete it.
I lift my arm and look at the mark on my ribs.
I use a nail.
I have to.
It is done.
It is perfect.
I must hide it.

'What's that?' Nick was peering at my ribcage. I quickly clamped my arms to my sides and made a show of scrubbing my thighs.

'Oh nothing, darling, I think I scratched it moving stuff in the stockroom yesterday. There's nails sticking out all over the place.' Shut up! I was telling myself. Shut up. 'You know what the back room's like, junk everywhere.' Not only was I not shutting up, I was talking faster and faster. 'God, you should have seen it, filled to the brim, it took for ever.' I turned my back to Nick and let the shower sluice off the soap.

It made a good job of the soap but did nothing to cleanse my guilt.

Nick came closer and tried to lift my arm up. I slithered out of the way. 'That tickles, Sweetheart. Really, it's nothing.'

'It had better be nothing.' He replaced the shower curtain and quietly left the bathroom. How could I have been so stupid?

Idiot

Idiot

idiot

It had been the first time I'd taken such a risk. I knew at the time I would get caught. I had thought the old 'I caught it on a nail' routine was a solid one but I knew I'd never pull it off. It was the direct lying I found difficult. That was real lying. That was bad. The thing was, it was partly true. I *had* been in the stockroom and I *had* scratched my side on a rusty nail sticking out of the wall and it *had* made a shape and it *had* been the shape of a love heart.

But the nail had only made half a love heart.

It was me and my implements that had made it a whole. I knew it I knew it I knew it. I knew at the time I would be caught out. The last thing I wanted was for it to be seen as 'a cry for help'. That was not what I wanted at all. I was a master at covering my tracks.

Why did I do it?

Idiot

Get in the middle of a food chain reaction

If I cut all the vegetables and put them in the pot and stir and stir and let it cook without eating any, I will get thin ankles.

So far so good.

I look up at the shelf to get the salt and catch the fork as it almost reaches my lips.

Nice try.

It takes strength but I put it down.

I cook the food and put it on the plate. Don't touch. If I taste it before I reach the table I will be fat for ever.

I manage a few steps. Then something tricks me and grabs my attention. It is only the fact that the curtain needs to be pushed back a little but it is enough. Before I know it I feel food, delicious hot sweet spicy thick strong food in my mouth and I chew it about three times and swallow. I have been trying to chew at least 15 times per mouthful recently but I've ruined it now anyway so it doesn't matter.

I'm going to be fat for ever.

So I eat it all and refill it and eat the refill on the way back to the table then go back and just pick up the pot and eat it from there until the pan is bare.

Fatness, fatness everywhere.

I had been going to psychotherapy for two months and had come up with the brilliant cover that I was attempting to sort out some remaining 'issues' I had with my absent father.

Everyone bought it. Even my Mum. When I told her about it she suggested that maybe it would help to talk to my Dad. She told me that she would support me through it and I knew how hard that would have been for her to say. I felt bad but maybe I could get through this without admitting the truth to anyone.

So I sat on my sofa and thought about food. Then I glanced at the fish tank.

Ahh, Pete, my little friend.

He had a pencil thin black moustache which made him look like he was trying just a little too hard to be grown up.

I loved him so much. He was so cute. He was a London Shubunkin and would bob proudly between my other two goldfish knowing full well he was my favourite but having the good grace not to let it show too much.

By day he was my happy little comical friend but at night he repulsed me. He would come to me in hideous sickening dreams where, after death defying leaps, I would have to rescue his convulsing slippery body from the carpet. Once I even dreamt he jumped into a pan of curry while I was cooking.

I began toying with the idea of telling my Mum the real reason I was in therapy. My survival mechanisms were beginning to break down. The more I entered into myself for that hour on a Friday morning, the more I felt them crumble away. I knew deep inside that I couldn't do it all alone. If I gave it just one more week, maybe I would be brave enough. I resolved to confide in her.

A few days later we met for lunch. I was nervous with the weight of what I had to tell her. We finished our food and my

Mum took my hands and looked deep into me. For a second I panicked.

She knows!

I slowed my breathing and felt sure she could hear my heart banging.

She leaned in further and quietly told me she had a sensation in her breast. I followed her dumbly through to the ladies and she let me look at it. I remember being faintly irritated when I saw her feebly pull her arm through a bra that was too small. I noticed there was no toilet roll, the light was flickering, someone had dribbled pee on the seat. And so it went on until I finally looked to the familiar flesh of my Mum's breast. Though this time, it didn't look so familiar. It was as though her nipple was being pulled and puckered by some invisible force. Her eyes flickered just enough to show me she was worried.

'I'll be fine.' She put her arms around my shoulders as we went back to our table. Whenever I started to talk about it she widened her eyes and raised her brows. Now was not the time. She *would* be fine. She paid the bill and we left the restaurant. I went my way and she went hers.

When I got home that very day, I noticed that Pete's wee slippery body had begun to bulge slightly on one side. Slowly, the lump got so big that his body began to bend in horrible angles. My dreams became unbearable marathons of rescuing and touching something that shouldn't be held. I would wake up feeling like my diaphragm was going to frisbee into my throat.

The bulge erupted later into a huge sore and Pete fought to stay upright, his wee fins flailing. I bought all the medicines – stress coat, special fish enzymes. I even quarantined him from the other two, though not for their benefit, I thought Pete could do with a rest.

My Mum's cancer was confirmed but it was my little fish that I cried for. He was dying in front of my eyes with a gaping festering wound eating him from the inside out until he was bent almost double.

I came home after work one day to find Pete's isolation tank empty.

'I'm sorry, sweetheart.' Nick put his arm around me. 'He didn't make it.'

But by that point I wasn't bothered.

The Devil has sent the ravens

I lie in my bed with the covers stretched tight over my mouth like a gag.

There's something at the window. It bangs and bangs and bangs. It's going to get in.

Bang

I don't want to see what form He has taken. I think my heart would stop and that would be it. If I look into His eyes at the moment I die, that's it; my soul will have gone. Lost for ever to the dark side.

Bang

I can almost see my heart jumping out of its cage. I clutch my arms to my chest to retrieve it.

Bang

Like someone you scream at in a horror movie, 'No, don't go! You'll die!' I feel myself getting out of bed pulled towards the noise and the source of my terror.

Bang

I am about to meet him face to face.

Bang

At last.

Bang

It has been an endless courtship.

Bang

I hold my breath tight into my lungs and squeeze my eyes shut.

Bang

What form has he taken?
Bang
I open the door and look at the window.
Bang
A raven crashes its lead beak again and again onto the glass, the noise is huge. Its eyes are bleeding. They bleed over the glass and look straight into me.
Bang
With the same air still splitting my lungs I run back and dive into my bed counting to twenty-five over and over again. If I count to twenty-five twenty-five times it will be gone.
Bang
If I make a mistake...
Bang
I will die

I believe I can fly

It was my Dad who made me believe I could fly. He would bring me sheets of paper and card and we would spend hours constructing wings to fit on my back. My favourite were the butterfly ones. He would cut out the shapes and I would decorate them with glitter and sequins and paint.

It was a real sensation. I always felt I should have had wings. I could feel it. I could feel it on the tips of my shoulder blades. They would tingle as if they were coming into bud. In the mirror at bath time I would round my shoulders and crane my head to see the evidence. I could never get a close enough look no matter how I pulled the skin. The angle was too awkward. But still I felt it. I wondered if my Dad felt it too.

Standing at the top of the small hill in my garden, I prepared for takeoff. My Dad counted me down.

'Three...' I felt a lightness come to my feet.

'Two...' Warmth and excitement filled my chest.

'One...' I felt a surge and I took off. My legs sprang me into the air and for an instant I flew beyond them. But only for a breath. The heavy clatter of my run carried me to the foot of the hill and I landed heavily at the bottom.

'You did it, I saw you!' My Dad's voice hit me in the back and slid off the wings that now hung around me in a lifeless cloak. I sighed.

'Really?' I turned my head and blinked at his silhouette on the crest of the hill. A breeze ruffled his hair, then he came on down towards me. My wings fluttered gently and nudged the feeling back into my shoulder blades.

'Okay, I'll try again.' I hoisted myself to standing and as I reached the top a skip had returned to my step.

'This time.' My Dad squeezed my arm.

'This time...'

Later, my Mum shared in our chatter as we embellished our flying story. I let myself get carried away. I let myself believe in their smiles.

But that night, doors still slammed.

Maybe if I flew for longer next time.

I cuddled my arms around myself and felt for my wing buds. I knew they were there, I just couldn't reach them.

Behind the curtains

The sun was streaming in on us as we waited for my Mum's name to be called.

I was whispering with my sister, Nadia, asking her if she thought my Mum was being too hasty demanding a double mastectomy, but I could see her mind wasn't quite focused and her eyes were looking slightly to the right of mine.

'My God, look at your spots! They're all down the side of your head.' I couldn't tell if she was avoiding my question or simply blocking it out.

'Well, I can't bloody see them from that angle,' I said. 'You could at least squeeze them for me.'

She pretended to gag.

Then my Mum's name was called. We gathered our things from the waiting room floor and followed her through to the consultation room.

We perched on our seats straining to hear what was going on behind the curtains. I remember they were blue and flowery. They fluttered as the consultant moved around the bed studying my mother's torso. She'd been told to strip to the waist. I hoped his hands weren't cold.

She was very proud of her breasts. She could balance a one pence piece on her nipples and was delighted when Robert Redford (a favourite) had once said, 'Happiness is a woman with freckles on her titties.'

I heard her wince from behind the curtain and began to recall why this felt so familiar to me. About four years previously my Mum had taken my sister and me into town to get piercings done. I started with my belly button and peeped through the curtain as Nadia had her tongue done.

My Mum, who was just there as chauffeur, observer and probable source of payment, ended up getting both her nipples pierced and proudly informed us that the experience had made the piercer's year!

She wondered later if these bars of metal could have contributed to the cancer.

After the examination was over, Mr Davidson, a consultant well respected in his field, sat back behind his desk and smiled. My Mum smiled hugely back and I suddenly felt embarrassed, worried that she had developed a crush alongside the cancer. My sister and I waited with stone faces for the diagnosis.

It was inflammatory breast cancer – the most invasive and quickly-spreading kind.

With the shock came disbelief.

With disbelief came drama.

With drama came adrenalin.

With adrenalin came euphoria.

Euphoria? What was I? I couldn't shake the feeling of excitement rising in my lungs and throat. I was jittery. I looked round at my Mum and sister expecting grief-stricken faces. They were on the same brink as me and we simultaneously snorted and giggled.

The giggle became a laugh.

The laugh became a belly laugh.

The belly laugh became sidesplitting and we held on to our ribs as tears sprang into our eyes.

The tears began to roll down our cheeks.

The tears became sobs.

The sobs became low hacking crying.

The crying rocked our bodies into one another's until we were hugging and supporting and being supported.

The chemo was to start straight away. Aggressive treatment for aggressive cancer.

'What about alternative therapies? I've been reading books in case it was the cancer,' my Mum asked hopefully.

The doctor looked her straight in the eye. 'I'm sorry, Ms Swan, of course it's your prerogative to try whatever you can alongside the conventional medicine, but if you don't start treatment now, your condition will be a lot more difficult to control.'

We knew what he meant.

The gravity of the situation began to spread through my head.

A time to type

Throughout my childhood and growing up my Mum had worked. She was a typesetter and would sit in front of her computer all day long, sometimes into the evening. She returned to work six weeks after I was born, though she hadn't wanted to. It was her lifelong dream to be surrounded by children, playing, cooking, educating. She only had me and my sister. There was five years between us. Five years of typing – that's a lot of words. I timed her once; on a marathon sitting she could do ten characters a second. That's thirty-six thousand an hour! She liked to have her neck rubbed or hair brushed while she worked. I would rub her neck for ages or put French plaits in her long highlighted red hair.

It was a few days after her first chemo. She said she felt brilliant. I took up my position behind her as she typed and started to rub her big broad shoulders, always solid with tension, and kneaded my thumbs into her freckled flesh. My fingers always caught on a thin silver chain she wore but I never got round to taking it off. She had a lump low in her neck on the right hand side like a wart. It was white and gristly and had always been there. Sometimes it made me queasy and I avoided touching it; other times I hardly noticed it under my hands.

We chatted about many things during these sessions but since the diagnosis, the main topic was the cancer and how weird it all was.

Whenever I said something like, 'But why you, Mum?'

'Why not me...?' she would reply.

Rubbing my Mum's neck and playing with her hair relaxed me too. I would fall into a fantastical dreamlike state in which I fantasised about the future or remembered things from the past.

It was an autumn day and the smell of November knocked me back into the November when I was thirteen. It was meant to have been the last time I saw my father.

*

My weight shifts from foot to foot as his eyes bore into me expectantly.

'Just tell me what I've done wrong?' His voice has an edge to it and I wince.

What have you done wrong? What have you done wrong? Where is my tongue? Where is my memory? I try to pluck a single droplet from the terrified sea in my mind. It flits through my fingers again and again.

I watch him pitifully as he rolls up his sleeve to reveal a plaster cast on his right wrist. I forbid myself to mention it. I will not feel sorry for him. Not on this day.

I feel my throat well and tears push into my eyelids. I push back my sorrow and whisper, 'We don't want to see you again, Daddy.'

His eyes turn wild and pale. The change is subtle but it is immense to me. His eyes, a perfect gauge. I can tell if it will be a good day or a bad day depending on these eyes.

These eyes throw me into the images and memories I need to pull strength from. I don't want to remember but I need to...

My little sister is running into my room. 'Daddy's here!' She speeds out and I fly after her holding onto her jumper until I can detect the mood the day will take. One look is all I need and I usher her quickly into the garden to play. I want to shut it all out but my ears remain pricked and alert.

We pull on our roller skates while the shouting and thumps seep through the windows and doors. My routine is well rehearsed. We go to the far end of the garden singing and skating while I glance back and push my Nadia forward. I have to keep us out of his way and my sister distracted. I'm smiling and joking but my heart is loud and fast and my voice keeps getting higher. Round and round we trip and fall and play until the time I fear most. He comes outside and calls me over. I tell my sister to keep playing.

He asks me to sit on his knee and he holds me close with shaking arms. His crying makes his glasses steam up. I stare at the ground and my blue roller skates. They are secondhand and the laces are frayed so much that you can't do them up where the eyelets are missing. They are the best things ever. I try to concentrate on them until I hear that he is repeating a question. Asking me to promise him something. I listen in terror while he asks me to promise him that, no matter what happens, he will give me away when I get married. I am kind of confused by this question but quickly realise how important it is. I look at him with wide innocent eyes and say, 'Of course, Daddy!' Then I start to cry. I feel so sorry for him because I know he won't. The guilt of knowing this is unbearable. His eyes are wild and watery and I feel heavy.

His eyes.

Suddenly I come to. He has been shouting and is standing too close. I am rigid and dumb. His eyes and voice weld together and double in force. I shrink to a tiny dot in the back of my head to get away from it all.

Eventually I make out his words that roar and spit. 'Don't you worry; I've got it all on record. I'm going to write a book and expose you all for what you've done to me!' Then he barges away. A silence engulfs me. Everything is soft. I finally breathe in and let my tight heart inflate as I look down at my sister.

We've done it.

I grab her hand and hold my breath again as I listen to his green Datsun grinding away down the drive. I can't look at it.

'Please be gone. Please be gone. Please be gone,' I repeat over and over until we get to the trees at the bottom of the driveway. I pull my sister close to me as I dare to look at the space where his car had been parked.

Gone.

I feel like I could fly home. With one sentence, the great weight of my childhood has been lifted from my shoulders.

*

I sighed and began to massage my Mum's hair at the temples. Fifty-one and her hair had never gone grey at all. Her strong shoulders and strong hair sent me back to my memories.

*

My back is to the car and I stand rigid with my eyes shut facing the sun. I will its searing rays to burn through me and kill me but I still breathe. I realise I am shaking and am thankful that I am one of the last ones out of school so hopefully none of my friends will see what's going on. I am hot inside my school uniform and I hear his shaking voice.

'Just give me five minutes, Lauren.'

Just five minutes.

I am absolutely terrified. He was waiting at the gate for school to finish.

The weight of a thousand bricks falls back into place on my shoulders. I feel my knees buckle under the strain.

I turn around and lean towards the window. Tears are already on my cheeks and I sniff as I say as brightly as I can, 'Hello, Daddy, what are you doing here?' I can't look him in the eyes.

I stare at the passenger's seat. Dusty stuffing pokes out through a hole roughly patched with Sellotape – the kind of hole which nips your bare legs when you sit on it. I thought this was over. What is he doing here? I thought they said we would never have to see him again. Out of the corner of my eye I notice a second car do a u-turn in the road and pull to a full stop directly behind his. My Mum blazes out of the driver's door and strides towards me.

'Lauren, get in the car.' I make a run for it, she follows. By the time I yank the door shut we are already moving. She barely checks the mirror as we pull out and around his car. The car lurches as she slams on the brakes. He is standing right in our path. He slams his hands down on the bonnet and I close my eyes and bring my knees up to my chest. *Just Drive Mummy*, I think over and over. *Just keep driving.* I hear a noise but everything sounds alien. I lift my head and look from my

Mum to my Dad and back again. Their faces are contorted and snarling. I am shaking. My Mum's fist is white on the steering wheel. I realise what the noise is – the horn. It is suddenly too loud and splits my ears. I shut my eyes again and wrap my arms around my head.

'Just drive,' I scream as loud as I can. 'Just run him over!' I am crying now. I feel the car suddenly move forward and an ear-cracking bang makes me freeze. What have we done?

'It's okay,' my Mum strokes my hair as we drive. 'Lauren, it's okay.' But I can't open my eyes. 'Lauren, look at me.' I turn my head towards her but keep my gaze low. 'Lauren please.' I lift my eyes and look past her. My stomach is spinning. Something catches my eye. The wing mirror next to my Mum is dangling by a thread with the glass shattered. It flaps pathetically against the car door. I can't see any blood on it.

'Did we kill him, Mum?' I hear a noise rise from my chest and I hold it inside me with my hands over my mouth. It swims around in my head. It is a disgusting animal noise.

'Lauren, Lauren, calm down!'

The car halts.

'My God, Lauren!' She is shaking me. 'Lauren, stop it. Stop it now!' Suddenly the noise stops and is replaced by spasmodic sniffing. I wipe my nose with my sleeve. 'Lauren, for God's sake, we didn't drive over him. He came round to try to get in and smashed the mirror off!' She soothes me some more. I look suspiciously at the window then at her face. Of course we didn't drive over him! Relief fills me and I find my nerves are making me laugh and cough at the same time. 'Lauren, please calm down, you're going to make yourself sick!'

And I do. I suddenly feel that odd welling sensation in my mouth and I am sick all over my schoolbag and the car. I feel strange but better and my Mum starts the car up and rubs my neck the rest of the way home.

'How did you know he was there?' I am so thankful my Mum came to my rescue. I feel like she must have super powers. When we finally get out of the car I run into her strong arms.

We hear a knock at the door and my Mum goes to answer it. I am expecting my sister and go to the kitchen for some juice. I hear a man's voice echoing through the house and I suddenly feel very tired. My Mum comes into the kitchen followed by a policeman.

'What's going on?' I ask, immediately panicking about my sister.

'We've had a complaint of a physical assault on a Mr David Walker.'

What? What? What? What? I feel myself shrinking into that tiny place at the back of my head again.

'Well, he says that you tried to run him over in your car in an unprovoked attack.' I feel furious and helpless. I have been in contact with the police many times. Phoning, begging for help, when windows were being smashed, and shouting and hitting and shouting and they would never do a thing.

Not a thing.

Domestic.

What were they doing here now with a lie? I feel exhausted. Shattered.

'He smacked our mirror! He came over to us and smacked our mirror. We drove off!' I am so angry I start crying. I think we are going to be arrested.

'Don't worry,' he says. 'I'm sure this will blow over.'

*

I looked at my hands; they were covered in my Mum's hair. I quickly shook them and the strawberry golden strands fell to the ground in disgusting wisps. I wiped my palms on my jeans and silently started rubbing again, my heart pumping. My fingers began to shake as the hair started coming out in clumps around them. I felt nauseous. I didn't want to tell her.

'What's the matter?'

I couldn't speak. I showed her my hands. There was a silence while she carefully studied them.

'Pass my brush.' I watched as she gingerly pulled the hairbrush through her hair, with her left hand following its path patting carefully like a man with a fragile comb over. The taste of tears was in my nose. My Mum saw this and glared at me with a 'Don't you dare' look in her eyes. I swallowed them down.

> *Something has changed.*
> *The body has become silent.*
> *Silent in movement.*
> *It no longer squirms inside its polythene prison.*
> *I go to touch it...*
> *My outstretched fingers tap it on the arm.*
> *Time passes.*

A twitch.

I saw it.

Satisfied for now, I push on the liquefying form until it is concealed again under the bed.

Toupee or not toupee

My sister, Mum and I were sitting in a row in front of the huge mirror with our chins tucked in and nostrils flared. The trio reflected back was a far cry from the glamorous models we had imagined we'd see.

'Remember the coconut monkey?'

We snorted giggles as we remembered the hideous souvenir brought back from some last minute package holiday. It was a creature based on a monkey carved from two coconut husks with a fibrous bob as its crowning glory.

So much for the Three Degrees.

'That's what we're like, three bloody coconut monkeys.'

'Bloody hear no evil, see no evil, speak no evil!'

We were trying on wigs. My Mum's hair had been reduced to a patchy fluff from being on chemo and she had a voucher from the NHS for a new do. We made light of it but as I glanced at her when she wasn't looking I could see the ache. She was a woman who took great care with her appearance, mostly at the expense of other drivers as she applied lipstick in the rearview mirror, oblivious to changing lights. She would spend a long time getting ready every morning and would never leave her room without lipstick and mascara, even to feed the dogs. She would get on our nerves by constantly asking, 'Do I look all right?'

'Yes! You look gorgeous!' Nadia and I always replied, rolling our eyes. It was the truth. She did.

Always.

She never believed it though so I wondered now how her self-esteem would cope with this double attack on her femininity.

I had clippered my own hair off in sympathy, though I had stopped short of completely shaving it. I regret that now.

Of the three of us sitting under the brutal fluorescent lights of the wig parlour, only my sister's beautiful dark mane remained, and by the time we'd stuffed it into the golden toupee her head was enormous.

It was the week before Nadia's 21st birthday and we were having a girls' day out – my Mum's speciality, especially if there was an event coming up, or one of us was celebrating good marks, or one of us was feeling low, or happy, or if we were just plain old skint and needed cheering up. In fact any occasion that could possibly be used as an excuse would be. It was brilliant, though always 'the last'! We had already bought our outfits for the fast approaching birthday celebrations and had celebrated early with a £5.65 three course special with cola at the Bar Napoli. We were regulars of the lunch menu special and whenever my Mum walked through the door there would be exclamations of 'Ahh beautiful Joyce!' in warm Italian accents. It was nice to be spoiled like this.

So now for the best bit. New hair! My Mum plumped for one blond and one brunette bob and handed the vouchers over.

'Do you think it's real hair?' Nadia looked a bit squeamish as we peeled off a parking ticket from the windscreen and put it with the pile on the floor behind the driver's seat.

'Nadia, we were told to wash them in Daz.'

On the night of the party my Mum took to her bed feigning

nausea as planned and Nadia called me in tears. 'Mum can't come, she's feeling sick. Of all the days.' The chemo seemed to have had little adverse effects so far, so this, to Nadia, seemed absolutely typical of our luck.

Nadia reluctantly left her at home and met up with Kitty and me in the pub.

'Where's your pals?' Kitty put a tray of drinks on the table and slipped back into her seat. 'I thought the whole crew was coming!'

'Yeah, they're supposed to be.' Poor Nadia looked desperately around the pub for all the friends she had been expecting and Kitty gave me a little wink. After our third drink and forty-five minutes she finally asked where the toilets were.

'Downstairs. Come on, I'll show you.'

I led the way, leaving Kitty to lift her mobile to her ear. Luckily, Nadia didn't notice that we had passed the ladies on the way to the stairs. We arrived at a frosted glass door in the basement. It was dark and I could hear muffled giggles and shuffling. I let Nadia go ahead of me and then shoved her through the entrance.

A roar of 'Surprise!' went up as all her friends, led by my Mum, greeted her. My Mum had decided against wearing either wig and her face and scalp shone in the flickering birthday candles.

She was stunning.

My sister's face crumpled as she was hugged and kissed by everyone.

The Operation

I started to run.

I was sure I had passed that sign for the chaplaincy once already. And there was that fucking Palliative Care ward again.

'Does nobody get thirsty in this fucking place?' All I needed was a can of Coke.

And a straw.

And a cure for cancer.

I had been there when my Mum came round from the operation. She looked like a giant baby. Her eyes sparked with drugs and all she wanted was a can of Coke. And a straw. As soon as I left the room to get it I wanted to be back inside beside her, holding her hand. I hadn't bargained on not being able to find a vending machine. It started to turn epic. One of the only things my Mum had ever asked me for. A can of Coke. And a straw. I ran and cried and stopped crying immediately. 'Stop feeling sorry for yourself,' I snapped into my own ears.

She hadn't wanted me to wait in the hospital while she was in theatre so I had gone to the pub. I had sat in the corner at a huge table drinking beers for five hours. I felt like it might be appropriate to cry; other people might cry, I was sure that this was serious enough to warrant sympathy. I couldn't cry though. I just didn't feel that bad. I went back to the hospital.

I finally pushed my way through the Staff Only cafeteria door. It was in darkness but over in the corner I spotted, at last, a Coke machine with the lights still on. I pulled at my pockets and scattered change over the floor. Mission accomplished, I ran back through the now familiar and somehow homely corridors clutching the can. It was too cold. She might get a headache. I held it under my jumper to heat it up a bit and tried not to shake it up too much.

By the time I got back to the room there was desperation in her eyes.

'Where were you? You've been ages.' She looked upset. I explained about the Coke.

'You shouldn't have bothered, I'd much rather have you here.' I felt visiting time ticking away.

Four bags of blood hung on tubes from under her arms and her chest was bound tightly. I stroked her hands and laced my fingers between hers. I wanted to feed love from my eyes into hers. I wanted to reassure her.

'Dr Davidson hasn't been in.' It wasn't a question. She looked disappointed. My heart ached for her. I had put her down as having a crush and now I realised it was much more than that. He had made her feel beautiful and important and his attention must have given her hope that she could still be desirable. Now he had done his job, it was finished. He never came back to check on her. It must have confirmed what she had feared all along. I felt sad and stupid for being so insensitive.

The blood clung to the inside of the bags. They had removed both breasts and all her lymph nodes. There had been a trace of cancer in her right breast as well as her left. She had been right to demand the removal of both after all.

She sipped the coke through the straw like someone with early Parkinson's, a slight creepy tremor affecting her every move. Her jaw hung as if it was too loosely secured to her head, even though her teeth were clamped shut. She lay back into her pillows and kept sinking. I thought she would never stop.

'Here, let me help.'

'No, it's fine.'

'Mum, let me, it will make a difference, please.' I was desperate to plump her pillows, tuck some support into the crook of her neck and make her more comfortable. But she didn't want me to. It absolutely filled my brain to see her like that. At night, no matter what I try, no pillow will take the weight of my head. I have to hold it up on an aching neck all night for fear of it just falling off. That's how uncomfortable my Mum looked. It upset me so much to see her supporting her own head just like I have to.

They'll never know.
The cuts are only tiny.
Pathetic really.
They could easily pass for cat scratches or thorns.
They are not the Chinese burn of barbed wire I crave.
But they will do.
For now.

Crystal Healing

The antique pine table was littered with bits of torn up paper numbered from one to forty-nine. I sat holding a crystal pendulum on a chain and my Mum leaned in, concentrating.

We were trying to predict the winning lottery numbers.

I placed the next number in line under the point of the swinging crystal.

'Will this number be a winner tonight, Saturday night on the British National Lottery?'

We'd tried to include all the variables; the last thing we wanted was to glean the winning numbers for the French Lotto a week on Thursday.

It took ages. At one point Nadia popped her head through the door. 'You're not still doing that crap are you?' she said, retreating with a look of disgust and a hint of terror. In our family we had a fear of all things spooky or occultish, but today my Mum and I had decided to swallow this fear in favour of winning five million pounds.

We had asked the pendulum easy questions to decipher which action meant Yes and which No.

'Am I, Lauren, a girl?'

The crystal started to swing round in a circle. I steadied it.

'Am I, Lauren, a boy?'

The crystal wobbled for a second then began to swing straight back and forth. We had our code.

As we went through the numbers, one by one, we were really surprised at how seldom the pendulum answered Yes. By the time we got to forty-one we had only five numbers revealed as winners. We began to look at each other excitedly; I felt my heart beating as we prepared to find the last winning number. I looked at my Mum, and her expression turned grave. She lifted her face and looked into my eyes. I knew she wasn't thinking about the lottery.

'I don't know why this is happening.' It was as if for the first time she recognised the injustice of it all.

'I know, Mum.' I put my hand over hers and her eyes focused back onto the cards.

'One more to find!' She regained her composure and was smiling again. 'Come on, magic number!' Neither of us mentioned what else we could have asked the pendulum.

Our nerves began to quake as the crystal said No to every single number until we got to forty-nine. We both knew that the odds of getting a Yes to exactly six numbers out of forty-nine was as unlikely as winning the lottery itself. If this last one came in, these numbers were solid gold.

I held aloft the magic chain.

'Will this number be a winner tonight, Saturday night on the British National Lottery?'

The crystal quivered and began to swing in a wide and definite circle.

We were going to win the lottery.

Elated, we sat amongst empty Chinese take-away cartons and chocolate wrappers waiting for the National Lottery to pronounce us Queen. We had been drinking wine and even

Nadia thought we had a chance. We'd wound ourselves up playing the old 'what will you buy first?' game and were more than a little tipsy as the drums rolled and the ceremony began. One by one the little balls popped out. Our knuckles whitened around one another's.

As the last number was announced we all lifted our wine glasses.
Not one matching number.
Not one.

Circles and circles

I was sitting on the brown bobbly wool chair again. It looked like wool but I think it must have been polyester or some other 1970's synthetic fibre. It was the kind of material that made me shudder if I thought about catching a raggy finger nail on it.

I felt my heart rate increase steadily while time passed as he waited for me to speak. I hated this bit.

'How are you?' My voice got higher until it squeaked the last word. I was mortified I'd asked the inappropriate question. I looked up with a glance that I thought was sheepish even though that was not what I was feeling. I was feeling so awkward I could once again, if I had had a carving knife, have happily cracked it through my ribs and embedded it in my heart. The problem with hurting yourself is that the vision of it is so delicious and so, so inviting that you forget that it actually does hurt.

Quite badly.

So badly in fact that sometimes it makes you even angrier than you were in the first place.

'Why do you feel you have to ask me how *I* am, Lauren?'

This was what frustrated me – these were always the kinds of questions he asked – ones that made me feel diabolically stupid. What happened to lying on a couch and being asked about my father? There was a couch over by the wall near the multiplying spider plant perched on the windowsill. I was never asked to lie on it. I wondered how ill you had to be to get promoted to the couch. I always felt exhausted in this room and a wee lie down probably would have done me a power of good, but he never asked me. I assumed that was that and sat in my crappy chair rolling up never-ending balls of snotty tissues.

I began to notice the customs within the stifling room, like the tissues were not on view until after I started to cry, possibly to create a positive atmosphere – start on the right foot. Then, when the tears did come, the pastel box would be offered at exactly the most appropriate time.

'Because it's polite,' I answered his question.

'Is that important to you?'

'Of course!' Where was he going with this? I was getting more and more tired with trying to grasp at strands of thoughts in my mind that I wanted to unravel. Every time I thought I could catch one it slipped between my pinched fingers and flitted off back into its knot.

There was always this crushing expectancy that I should choose a topic to explore when I just wanted him to start me off. All my life I have been terrified of people reading my thoughts but now I was silently imploring this man. I just could not get my mouth to speak. Everything in there felt fake, pathetic, unworthy. I wanted him to do the delving and connect things up, tell me how awful I must feel, that I would be better soon.

'My Mum's got cancer,' I said to him.

'How do you feel about that?'

'I don't know. Upset, I suppose. Excited, maybe. No, I don't know.'

'Why excited?'

'Because, she might die. Why am I excited? I feel so bad. I was going to tell her about the real reason I come here. I was just about to say, then she...'

'Just about to say what?' he interrupted. I knew instantly what he had done and I was shocked back into my shame. He wanted to hear me say why I came here.

It was the first question again.

He wanted to know my expectations. I have never, ever, been able to voice my expectations of people. If my expectations were too high, I might make that other person feel bad or they might tell me to know my place.

'I was about to tell her the real reason I come here.'

'What *is* the real reason you come here?'

'Because...' you know why, it's on the report sheet, 'because I do things to myself.'

'Why?'

'I don't know.' We were going round in circles and my main fear was that if I didn't start talking soon, he would really think me unworthy of this attention and take my one hour slot on a Friday morning away from me.

'I'm angry with her.' There, I said it. It came out. I said it. Now it's true. Now I'm bad.

'Why?'

'I don't know...It's trivial and pathetic.'

'What is?'

'I feel like I never get space, I'm crushed in by her. On the one hand, she is the perfect mother; she gives me all the support and freedom in the world but when I am with her she is stuck to my side. She follows me into the bathroom and I'm like, "What the fuck are you doing in here?" It lashes the inside of my skull. I can't stand it. I feel so cruel and unreasonable.'

'Sounds reasonable to me.'

'What, that she should want to follow me everywhere?'

'No, that you should be angry.' I looked up and felt tears tightening my throat yet again, but this time it was not tears of self hatred, anger or sorrow. I was grateful for his understanding.

'It is reasonable to want your own space in the bathroom. It is also reasonable that you want your own space to explore yourself and get well.'

He'd done it. He'd given me justification and permission to be there, in that room, talking to him. At last, weeks of not knowing what to talk about suddenly transformed into eloquent streams of monologue queuing up to be heard. I opened my mouth to set it free but just as I was about to speak I caught his eyes glancing up at the clock.

I sealed the gates and kept quiet until the second hand reached its destination.

The hint

What could I do?

What could I do with my life?

I wanted to help people. Love people. But I had come to the realisation that I couldn't. I couldn't because I held no space in my being for love for myself. I knew I could be witty, I knew I was creative, I was good at dancing and singing, but I just didn't love myself. I could admire things about my personality fairly objectively, but not passionately.

So what could I do?

I reluctantly admired myself for admitting to the doctor that I had a problem that I could not conquer by myself. Wow. That was a blow. The realisation that I was slipping out of my own control and having to *ask* for help to grasp myself back. That the super human powers I believed I had were obsolete in this task.

So what could I do?

I needed to get away from the country, myself, all this confrontation I was confronting in myself, the battle I was fighting and keeping hidden from all my family and friends. I was a master of disguise. A shadow warrior.

I felt alone.

I was on the bus. The number 10. I had just left my therapy. I had developed a routine on Friday mornings; I would get off at M& S to get a cappuccino and cheese scone and take it over to Princes Street gardens. And then I would sit and sit and think. I pictured myself with my treats and knew I would be late for work…guilt started its spraining journey yet again but I remembered old Charles's words. 'Take as much time as you need. I can handle things here.' So I tried to switch my thoughts to something else and picked up a discarded Metro newspaper.

And there it was…

On the very first page I opened.

'Walk across the Namibian desert in support of the Maggie's Centre.' The page shone; the picture was perfect. A long beautiful sky with mountains of sand dunes. Escape. Escape with meaning and a connection. I could hardly wait to tell everyone. I could see myself valiantly up at the front of the leading pack (of course) sipping gratefully on crisp water from a personalised hipflask. I would wear khaki shorts and a muslin shawl which would billow romantically around me. Tanned muscles pumping – not a hint of body hair. It would all be so perfect. I would be escaping on the back of raising money for Maggie's, a place where cancer patients and their families could go and find comfort from books or counsellors or other patients and their families. I had passed it every single day that my Mum had been in the ward since the operation. It was a modern brick and glass building and looked intriguing. I had never gone in though.

The bus arrived at the scone stop and I jumped off with a delighted skip in my step. I breathed in cold air and let myself feel my excited heart jump a beat. I was thrilled at my plan. I knew it was going to happen! I almost felt too excited to eat but quickly told myself not to be so stupid; I am always able to eat. I would just be full of regret and hunger if I didn't. If

I did, I would just be full of regret. That's the way it works. It distracted me for a minute but then I remembered my plan.

> *Where?*
> *Something catches my feet as I run.*
> *Slippery little hands grab me.*
> *They slow me down.*
> *My footsteps are stuttery and clamped.*
> *Now I am slipping on plastic.*

The hills are alive

The hall was packed.

All the would-be adventurers, including myself, had gathered in the main room of the place we would be raising money for.

The Maggie's Centre. It was the first time I had been through its doors. It was too intimidating. They might have told me I wasn't allowed in. They might have told me my Mum's cancer wasn't serious enough for the privilege. I left my seat to check out the toilets. I didn't need a pee, but I did need to get away from the throng. It buzzed with the word cancer, cancer, cancer. I felt numb to it and sat on the toilet imagining how I might introduce myself to them all.

'Hi, I'm Lauren.' Dazzling smile. 'I'm walking on behalf of my Mum Joyce who has inflammatory breast cancer.' Another dazzling smile to show how brilliantly we are all coping, then a brief background of my fitness levels punctuated with quick-witted little jokes to show them I would be a strong and good fun member of the team. I scanned the posh little bathroom with its Crabtree and Evelyn rose liquid hand soap (do they fill it with Tesco's own when it has run out?) and its cancer pamphlets. I picked one up, read the first sentence and quickly put it back.

Back in the hall, I squeezed into my seat. Everyone had shining eyes and friendly open faces. It was the kind of friendly and welcoming atmosphere I had always longed for and tried to create.

I still felt like I didn't belong.

The room was brought to order by the man who would be leading us on the trek. It sounded amazing, exhilarating and exhausting. We would walk one hundred miles in ten days over the Namibian desert. I started to get really excited as the leader talked us through slides of previous years' expeditions. After a talk about footwear, hygiene and sleeping arrangements we went on to the most important topic: We each had to raise £2500 to secure our place on the walk. The group shared their ideas for fundraising; a sponsored carwash, a car boot sale, someone shaving her head, men dressing as women for the day etc. etc. Charles had given me loads of old stock and I had arranged a Books and Booze night in the pub opposite the shop. I handed out invitations to my fellow trekkers.

The money ideas were soon exhausted and we all turned our attention to the white football our leader was carrying. While he held it he told us a bit about himself and why he had got involved with this project, then he threw the ball randomly to a man in the room. Davy, 36, brother diagnosed with testicular cancer. He would be ballroom dancing down his high street to get the sponsorship. Then Diane, a hairdresser, sister with leukemia, would be doing a haircutathon. I practised my speech as the ball was passed from person to person, each one with a story. Some joked, some cried, some were too shy and just said their name. I was excited for my turn and finally caught the ball.

'Hi, I'm Lauren,' my voice started to shake. I swallowed. 'My Mum has just had a double mastectomy.' I burst into floods of tears and dropped the ball. There was silence, then, 'There, theres', and, 'Never mind, it's a bit overwhelming.' I nodded through my hair and mucus and they threw the ball to someone else.

But my speech. . .my debut! I'd been rehearsing!

It was too late. Jimmy, 47, plumber from Aberdeen, had the ball.

The Burn

I had been staying a lot at my Mum's house while she was recuperating. Not only to help her but to offer support to my sister who had been the main carer throughout her illness.

I had started training in earnest, that is, not just imagining myself running and how brilliant I would be, jogging for miles with Hollywood sweat patches under each arm and down my back. Long walks around the sprawling countryside where my Mum and sister lived had made me feel I was definitely getting fitter, but I got quite bored with no one beside me to bring out my competitive streak. Slowly but surely, my Mum was getting stronger and one day she asked to come along as my training partner. I wondered if it was too much for her but she insisted and I was delighted. She cycled beside me along the country road and I ran; our goal was the woods about a mile away. She was in leggings and yellow clogs and the bike chain had only popped off twice so far.

'I wish I was coming with you, Laur.'

I felt myself cool.

'I always dreamed of going to Africa.'

My t-shirt suddenly felt wet against my back.

'I know, Mum. I wish you could come too.' The lie slipped easily over my panting tongue. Every BBC wildlife programme we had watched as children would have my Mum telling us that she had always felt like a tigress and how she wished she could prowl across the African plains. Live Aid had her desperate to go out and feed those starving babies herself. I felt my shoulders dipping. I felt my excitement turn to selfishness. *I want it for me! It's mine! You can't come.*

My Mum had some rich clients and together we had easily raised the sponsorship target. I was glad the deadline for new entrants had passed. I shut out the guilt and concentrated on the running.

I was determined to make it to the forest without stopping and to my utter amazement I did! I paused at the trees, hands on thighs, to relieve the burn in my lungs. I let saliva slide out over my teeth and gums onto the road. My Mum was staring at me intently.

'You seem a bit weak, sweetheart.' Her eyes looked concerned. *What? But I ran the whole way!*

I thought I had said it out loud but my mouth was still closed trying to hold in my aching teeth. Why would she say that when I'd just run the whole way?

> *'Sweetheart, try to remember.' Nick gently guides me through to the bedroom where the body still lies, the bag clinging to breasts and thighs.*
>
> *I back into him. 'We have to tell somebody!'*
>
> *'No.' His grip tightens round my upper torso, my arms pinned to my sides. 'Lauren, we've already been over this. Your Mum's coming over with the car and we're going to dump it.'*
>
> *'My Mum knows?'*

I watched my Mum and sister from the lawn where I was mucking around with some old golf clubs and balls. They were sitting at the garden table, chatting, Horace the Dobermann was being a pain. My Mum bent down and gently swiped him on the head. I could hear Nadia laughing and it was a beautiful day. I looked at the ball.

I looked at my Mum's head.

I looked at the head of the club.

I looked at the dog's head.

I swung my club as I focused on the huge bay window just behind them. In slow motion the ball sailed through the air straight through the window next to my Mum's head.

I couldn't believe I did it. My lungs stopped moving and I held my mouth in my hands.

Why did I do that? It was completely deliberate.

'Lauren. You meant that!' my Mum shouted.

'Well, not really. I was aiming for your head.'

'Thanks very much!' my Mum laughed. 'Good shot! You were bloody close!'

'Mum, I'm really, really sorry. I don't know why I did that. I'll pay for the glazier.' I ran over to her, feeling white and confused. I did not understand myself.

'Don't worry, I need to get new glass on the hob anyway. I'll get it done at the same time.' I couldn't believe this woman. I had just missed her head by millimetres with a golf ball, smashed her huge bay window and she wanted to pay for the damage.

I went in to survey the scene.

I knelt in the living room looking at the mess I had caused. I started to clean up the glass all around me. As I fingered the shards I felt my breathing increase and I quickly checked over my shoulder. I pulled up my trouser leg and dragged a sharp edge over my skin, pulling it deeper as it crawled further up my leg. I loved the way a cut done with a sharp blade wouldn't bleed for a few seconds, as if in shock, then it would panic and wouldn't stop. This wasn't stopping. It bled and bled. I was euphoric.

I had cut myself.

I could show my family.

I had the perfect excuse.

'How did you manage that?' My trousers were still rolled up when I passed my Mum carrying the glass wrapped in newspaper.

'I knelt on a bit sticking in the carpet.' I felt awful and sick for lying but thrilled that it was such an easy bluff. I pottered around her trying to act normal while feeling a bit nervous and sweaty. I ran through beginnings of light, silly conversations I just couldn't force through my lips. I felt her eyes on me.

'You did that deliberately.'

'The window, I know. I'm so sorry.'

'No, the cut.' Her eyes looked like they were finally begging me to come clean. Reaching out to me. Ready to help me.

It was the moment I had been waiting for all my life.

I couldn't stand to see her pain. It terrified me.

'Don't be silly, Mummy...' I smiled and gave her a hug.

> *Just you wait.*
> *I'm going to tell on you.*
> *I will.*
> *I will.*
> *Just you wait.*

Better, ta-da!

'So this is the last session we can offer you, Lauren.' Time had never passed so quickly and so slowly.

The last year stretched itself out in my mind like chewing gum in a languid 50 session epic, and then flashed by in bursts of oncologists, operations and chemo.

'How do you think these therapy sessions have helped you, if at all?' Graham looked at me, his elbow on the armrest and two fingers pressed into his cheek.

'Good, yes. I'm feeling good.'

'Can you elaborate?' He brought both his hands together under his chin and interlocked his fingers.

'Well, I don't hurt myself any more. I don't make myself, you know... any more.' I looked around the room where I had shared the most intimate spaces of my mind: the dreams, the nightmares, the actions, the hurt; and I felt a pang of fondness for the woodchip and spider plant and brown carpet and shit curtains.

I felt panic rising and looked away from Graham. I had always been quite blasé when he had tried in previous sessions to bring up the imminent end of my therapy. I believed that I would be relieved to see the back of the place.

'We will take an assessment of your progress and see if you need any further treatment.'

'I'm fine. I feel this has been a big help.' I felt I had only scratched the surface and was being abandoned. I wouldn't tell him that though.

He handed me the assessment form.

'The thing is, it may take a while to arrange further psychotherapy and it would almost certainly be with another practitioner.'

'I'm fine. Really.' There were people who needed this far more than me, I had pushed my luck enough already. I took the lid off the pen and placed crosses on the positive side, but not in every box.

I knew how the test was scored.

'So,' I handed the sheet of paper back. 'It was nice meeting you, Graham.'

My voice was strained. We, no, I had shared so much and now I felt ridiculous. I imagined this was how it would feel to wake up with a stranger after a one night stand.

I looked at the clock and started to gather my things together on my lap. As I started to get up, Graham motioned me to sit down.

'Lauren, I want you to know something.' His eyes were sincere and kind. 'I will be thinking about you. You will occupy space in my mind. Everything you have talked about and explored here is not trivial or unimportant to me. You will be remembered.'

I could have hugged him. My foolishness was washed away. I felt I was ready for the world.

'Thank you, Graham.' I shook his hand. 'Likewise.'

What if I just take a peek?
What if I just unzip it?

Just a tiny bit...
I could see who it is.
I would know.
Maybe I could fix it.

We were on the top deck (my choice) and at the very front (my choice). Nick sat next to me and was teasing me about how only complete saddos sit on the top at the front.

'It's not normal. These seats are for geeks and children.'

Every time we were on a bus together it was the same, but I couldn't bear the waste and claustrophobia of the lower deck. Why would you rather sit downstairs unable to see through windows thick on the outside with traffic film and thick on the inside with the condensation from the coughing breath of people too ill or old to get up the stairs? It drove me crazy.

Just look out of the window at what you'd be missing, Nick. You're never this high up. You can see everything. The familiar response to the familiar argument droned around my head just a little away from the real words I knew I had to speak. He was relaxed and easy after the film we had seen and if it had been anyone else they would have been chatting but Nick was making considered, jokey but clever remarks. I was sitting next to him with every part of myself rigid.

It was unbearable.

The bus swayed round a roundabout but I stayed upright and uptight. It crossed my mind that once when I had been riding on the back of a very fast motorbike I had been complimented on what a good pillion I was and how this was the complete antithesis of that. The thought was a deliberate distraction and I tried to shoo it away.

'Nick...'

I thought I'd spoken but I hadn't. For an instant I was relieved but then I was dipped back into my pressure sealed world. I had to do it now. I could feel the world turning around me, away from me. I had to get on it now.

It was time.

'Nick...?'

'What is it, darling?' He turned to face me with such intensity I knew he knew there was something wrong. 'What's the matter?'

The impulse to tell him nothing, I was fine, was almost overwhelming. Almost but not quite, my survival instinct had been kicked into action and I knew what I had to do if I wanted to get better. I knew that if I told him now I would never ever be able to do anything to myself again. It was scary. My old friends begged me to stay with them. My arms and thighs ached for the soothing knife. I wanted to retreat and be purged. But at last my heart managed to push them to one side.

'You know I've been going to psychotherapy, darling?' I hadn't told anyone the sessions were now finished. I still needed those two hours to myself on a Friday morning.

'Yes, are you sure you need to?' He twisted in the seat and hung his arm on the head rest. 'You know, I've been thinking about it and everyone has had some sort of problem in their childhood or with their Dad at some point, maybe it's time to let it go. It might be better to just leave some things alone. You've been getting worse since going there.'

'No, Babe, I'm getting better.' I paused and tried to look him in the eyes but settled on just below his chin. 'But it's never been about my Dad. Believe me. And believe this; you must believe that no matter what I tell you, I will never do it again, I promise.'

'What is it?' He looked scared.

'I have visions of stabbing myself and I feel fat and disgusting and I . . .'

'What? You don't cut yourself, do you? Is that what the mark was on your side? That scratch, did you do that to yourself?' He looked disgusted, angry and ashamed.

'Please, you must believe me. I will *never* do it again, I promise. Please. . .'

I looked at him properly, straight into his eyes. I needed to know he believed me and I needed to know how angry he was. I looked and knew that he was sad and worried but not angry. I wasn't sure if he believed me though.

'Is there anything else?' Now for the most shameful part, I thought. I thought maybe I'd shared enough and I could get away without telling him the rest. But if I didn't tell him I might do it again.

I didn't want to do it again.

'I have an eating disorder.'

'You're anorexic?'

I bowed my head.

'No, worse.' I started to cry and he pulled me in tight. His arms wrapped around me three times and his coat enveloped me in warm darkness. I felt my heart thundering again, a thundering I had felt so often, driven by rage and adrenalin, but this time instead of feeling lonely I felt Nick's heart beat with the same intensity as mine. I felt that I could conquer it now.

I felt Nick's neck craning round to look towards the back of the bus. Was he worried that anyone had heard? But then I felt his body lift mine up and support me as he rang the bell.

We had reached our stop.

We had reached our beginning.

The egg

I was early.

I am usually early.

Most people are late and think that fifteen or twenty minutes is acceptable. They do not realise that twenty minutes late equates to a forty minute wait to a twenty minute early person.

I was also grumpy.

I had a strange niggle in my back and felt faintly nauseous, all of this drowned by an extreme tiredness. Had I overdone it yesterday? No, I had had an early night and not even a drink. Maybe my period was due, that would explain the mood. I checked the clock and decided I could afford to be ten minutes prompt. My watch is fast, I could explain.

I climbed the three flights of narrow stairs to knock on the door of my potential new home. As the door opened I was greeted by a damp smell and a dour face. The curtains, still drawn at a north facing window, were ill matching and just too short, accentuating the lack of light which would have been able to get in had they been fully open.

This was by far the worst flat I'd viewed. I could barely feign interest as I asked the price. £450 per month plus a month in advance and £500 deposit. I asked whether the stained mattress propped up behind the door would be removed and the curtains changed.

No.

I left.

As soon as I got in my car I burst into tears. I cancelled my remaining two appointments and called Granny June.

By the time I had driven to her house all I could do was lie down on the cosy carpet in front of her hissing gas fire.

Granny June had prepared the usual feast of homemade soup with a potato extravaganza of shepherd's pie and chips to follow. But for once I had to refuse. I lay back down and fell asleep.

I was hardly even aware that a neighbour popped round for coffee at some point. I kept drifting in and out of sleep as blankets were arranged over me and hot lemonade, a Granny cure all, was left at my side to tempt me.

I came round about three o'clock in the afternoon, starving.

'Wow, Gran! Don't know what happened there!'

My back still groaned but the sleep had seemed to sort me out a bit. I tucked into my lunch.

Ten minutes later I was clinging to the toilet, throwing up as my body rejected everything. I tried to drink some water but with the same result. Granny June asked if it was a hangover.

Then I began to sweat. I soaked all my clothes and had to wear my Gran's nightie. That night I went through three sets of jammies and sheets. My Granny was there the whole time washing and drying as I tried to sleep.

I started shivering.

I started hallucinating...

I must hang on to this egg.
The egg.
The egg.
                    Is it really a stone. . . ?
                         Stop drifting. . .
                              can't stand it. . .
                                   hold the egg.
My arms can't reach round it but I must hold on. I must use all my concentration and hold on. The light will channel out through the top – but only if I concentrate on the egg. I must hold on. Don't look up at the light; it will only disappear.
Stop,
       just
             concentrate. . .

I had arrived at Granny June's on a Monday. Now it was Thursday and all I could remember about those fevered days was my egg. My granny must have changed me about forty times.

Nick was working double shifts at the pub and when he had phoned, I think I told him hazily not to worry.

It was on Thursday that it was decided I should go to the doctor. I remember a phone call with my Mum; I remember trying to tell her how I felt, how I was shaking from head to toe but really all I wanted was to get back to my egg.

I passed the phone back to my Gran and felt my vision tunnel. I heard her speaking into the phone and it felt like she could have been on a different planet.

'What's a doctor going to do that I'm not doing here? I'm taking good care of her.'

The Device, The Devil & Me

It hit me.

I needed a doctor.

In my Gran's local surgery I shook and shook and my bum bones rattled off the wooden chair. I looked up at the posters warning patients about various symptoms and just couldn't make sense of the images.

'Is that a telly or a poster, Gran?'

'What are you talking about, Lauren, you doughnut?' My Gran nudged me and must have thought I was making a joke because she was smiling at the time.

'No, Gran, it's moving like a telly but it doesn't have any switches.'

She held my hand and said, 'They're posters, darling. Come on, let's see this doctor, eh?'

In the consulting room the doctor asked me to stop shaking while he examined me.

'Em... I can't.' I think I even managed to roll my eyes. He said it couldn't be my kidneys because I didn't wince when he tapped my back. He took a urine sample anyway since he couldn't think of anything else. Sure enough, it was a kidney infection and I was given antibiotics. But the pills didn't seem to kick in and by Saturday my Mum called the emergency doctor.

Granny June insisted I put on new pyjamas and go through to her bed.

The other room was freezing. I was changed into yet more nylon nightwear. The sheets and covers were made of the same stuff and I slid about the bed worrying about static electricity.

'Oh yes. You're very weak. Your blood pressure is too low.'

The doctor looked to my Mum. 'Try to get her to eat something – even clear soup would make a difference.' She wrote a prescription for different antibiotics.

'I'm supposed to be walking the Namibian desert in two weeks.' I looked at the doctor and gave what I thought might have resembled an optimistic smile. It hadn't even occurred to me that this little hitch would stop me.

'You're not going anywhere, I'm afraid. Weakened kidneys can be very serious, especially in the desert.' I was devastated. I was so tripped out by my illness that I had been treating it as a bit of a joke – a skive from work in Granny June's cosy house. I had had no idea there might be repercussions.

My Mum decided to take me to her house to recuperate. It was in the car on the way there that she posed the question that I had been dreading.

'Maybe *I* could go in your place?' Sparkling eyes betrayed my Mum's concerned expression.

No, No, No – It's my thing I want to go. Me me me. Don't ask me the one question I can't say No to.

But she had.

'Would you be strong enough?' I asked quietly with my eyes to the floor.

Of course she would.

This was her dream.

> *'What do you mean, my Mum knows?'*
>
> *I am horrified. How could he tell her? I am so angry and ashamed I want to rip open the bag and stab the body some more.*

> *'How could you tell her? How could you?'*
> *'I didn't tell her, Laur. She's your mother. She knows.'*

I was staring again at myself in the big downstairs bathroom mirror while my Mum was lying on her side in front of the fire, leaning her head on her arm, watching telly. There was only a wall between us but there was so much more to wade through before I could reach her, reach out to her.

'Mum, I need to talk to you. . .' Every time I rehearsed my opening line the pamphlet would appear before my eyes and I would read it from memory, word for word. 'Do not burden a cancer patient with your own problems; they are going through a much bigger and more challenging journey.'

I so wished I had never read it.

I tried to blank out the pamphlet and told myself how my Mum would be far more devastated if I didn't talk to her. I could rationalise this very easily. My Mum wasn't the kind of cancer patient the pamphlet was talking about. She was my Mum. She would hate to be referred to as the cancer patient.

But still, by the time I had my hand on the door handle, I had stretched the skin back over my forehead and lifted my face into a smile. The unused adrenalin left me shaky and nervous and buoyant. I opened the door and bounced onto the sofa, then got straight back up.

'Fancy a cup of tea?'

Anything to get out of the room before she noticed I was acting strangely.

> *'Nick, why won't you let me tell the police?' I am so bewildered by the whole thing. I can't even remember*

doing it. 'Nick, she'll have family, people who love her, they need to know.' The more I say these things, the more they start hitting home. I can hear a thumping noise in my ears and nausea overwhelms me. I am on my knees with my arms round Nick's legs. I know I am crying because his jeans are hot and wet.

'Believe me, Lauren, they don't need to know this. It's too awful.'

He pulls his legs free from my grip and I crumple to the floor alongside the body. I don't even know who she is. My hand is shaking as I reach out to her face. I can't make out her features behind the bag, but she seems familiar. Panic starts to overtake me again. I pull back my hand and put it by my side.

It was on the third evening of convalescing at my Mum's that I decided to tell.

My sister was away on a cruise with her fiancé and so there was nothing to distract me from what was between my Mum and me. I'm not sure how it worked out really. I can't decide which part of me had given in first, my body, or my mind.

I was once again in the kitchen making yet more tea while trying to reabsorb the fight or flight chemicals jumping about inside me. I had once again almost started my speech but had chickened out at the last second. I was so angry at myself. As I stirred the teabags round in the pot, I took out the hot spoon and pressed it into the back of my hand. It was hot, but not hot enough.

I lifted the kettle...

I had no idea a human body would be so heavy. My hands slip and fumble as I try to heave it out from under the bed. The bag stretches and the blood inside slips over flesh. I gag. My hands feel weak, as if I have been sitting on them for an hour, turning them numb.

I am aware of voices. Nick and my Mum are standing behind me telling me to stop.

'No, Lauren. Don't look. Let's just get rid of it. Stop!' I shrug violently to reject the hand on my shoulder as I find the top of the zipper.

And then I stopped myself.

I took another deep breath and walked through to the living room.

She smiled at me as she always did, as though she hadn't seen me for years and had been waiting for this reunion.

'I need to tell you something.'

She pushed herself up to a sitting position and told me I could tell her anything.

'I hurt myself.'

At once her arms engulfed me and she asked if there was anything else.

'Yes.' My eyes stared at the floor as I prepared to admit my shame. 'I make myself sick.' She held me and we cried. She felt stronger than ever pressing me to her.

'Why didn't you tell me? Why couldn't you tell me?'

'I didn't want to disappoint you.'

'You could never disappoint me. I adore every part of you.'

'I wanted to tell you.' I told her about the cancer pamphlet.

'Oh fuck the cancer! It's you I care about. A pamphlet? What time we've wasted, what time we've wasted. I knew there was something wrong. I should have just asked you.'

Once again, I felt my burden lift.

I'm in the back of my Mum's car, peering out of my own head. My eyes feel strange like I can't physically move them but I can still see all around.

My Mum looks upset. She's very pale and her jaw is rigid. I stare at the twitching sinews in her cheek. Nick sits beside her. They aren't talking.

It isn't raining but I wish for the sound of the window wipers to soothe me.

Something isn't right.

I go to reach over and switch on the wipers but nothing happens. Nothing at all. I have not moved a single muscle. I have the will to move but my body will not obey. I am stuck in a body that will not function.

I start to panic.

No raised heartbeat or adrenalin backs it up. Am I panicking at all?

I wonder what is going on. I wish my Mum and Nick would tell me. I wish I could ask them. I have tried to speak but can't even inhale, let alone force breath over my throat. Suddenly, I realise. Neither of them is speaking but they are telling me. I can feel vibrations coming off them in waves reaching in and around me.

I am dead.

Dead.

They think I am dead.

They are taking me somewhere to bury me. Why aren't they taking me to the morgue? Where is my funeral? This doesn't make sense. Why would they just take me and bury me?

I don't feel dead.

I try desperately to communicate with them but they drive on.

Is this what happens?

Your body dies then all you are left with is yourself? For ever?

I can't stand it. I don't want to be alone for the rest of my life in the ground, watching the blackness, feeling nothing.

I stay sitting for a while, which is of course all I can do. I thought there would be some sort of explanation, a revelation. My Mum and Nick are sobbing. Their guilt and grief form layer upon layer of blankets around them. Thick and deep.

We are at the chosen spot now.

The hole has been dug.

For me.

This is it.

I scream with all my might.

'I'm not dead. I'm NOT DEAD! See me! Hear me! I am NOT DEAD!'

It's too late. Everything's over so quickly. I am in the hole. How have I died? How can I face this loneliness for ever?

I watch them staring down at me. They begin to drop

the first handfuls of earth on me. Something amazing happens. I feel it! I feel soil hitting my actual body. But every sharp blow of earth pierces my flesh and fragments of my soul begin to escape.

I can see it! It's like wisps of spun sunlight. It is beautiful.

I am beautiful.
I am beautiful.
I am free...

I allowed her to take care of me. I allowed her to mother me and I absorbed myself back into being her daughter. I felt happy and content, happy and content enough to put my battle on the shelf for a while. I managed to pare down my self attack to the bare necessities – that is, my praying ritual in the darkness before I could sleep. Eventually, with my Mum's reminders, I called the Maggie's Centre and told them she would be taking my place on the hike. They were sympathetic about my not being able to go and amazed that my Mum had taken up the baton.

Oh and she had.

With gusto.

She took her dogs on three walks a day over the fields and I tried to match her grin as she came back through the door all windswept and bubbling. I still clutched my crochet blanket around myself and wobbled a bit.

'Oh, this is going to be amazing. I'm so excited, so, so excited!'

I was glad I could hide my growing resentment behind my frailty.

Over the next ten days, after all the arrangements and rearrangements had been made, I phoned Kitty and told her about my feelings towards my Mum. I had never felt like this before. On the one hand I was pleased that she would be realising a dream; on the other, it was also *my* dream and I was jealous. There, I admitted it.

Jealous.

A horrible word for a horrible thing. But it was more than that. Letting her go in my place was like admitting that this was her last chance to do something like this. It was like facing up to the fact that she was going to die. I felt awful.

Then Kitty said something wonderful. 'Look, it's truly great for your Mum that she's going, but any show of excitement on her part feels like gloating. It's okay for you to feel bad. Sometimes the most precious things to give are those hardest to give up.'

I put the phone back into its cradle.

There.

I could breathe again.

The jealousy leaked away and was replaced with overwhelming joy that I had played a part in giving this woman a dream; a woman who had never begrudged anything she ever gave to anyone. And never took.

My hugs and kisses at the airport were completely genuine. She took my hand, squeezing hard, and stared deep into my eyes. 'Thank you,' she whispered, close to tears.

Doorways

It starts with a feeling.

A sensation of someone watching you, or creeping up on you. You try to be quick and spin round to catch them out but they're gone.

You're scared to spin round because the worst thing would be to see it. But you have to do it.

I spin...

He's gone. He must have jumped in front of me.

I spin back...

Gone again. Fear turns to anger and I grab my hair in two big fistfuls on the crown of my head and pull down towards the ground. I pull so hard that I wrench my neck.

Shit.

I've made a space.

It's a prime site right between the second and third vertebrae.

I've got to patch it up.

He's going to get in again...

My Mum was in Namibia and I was in the shop.

Now my secret was out, the rules had changed.

I could never hurt myself again. Now that the people I loved knew, I wouldn't just be hurting me, I would be hurting them.

I wouldn't do that.

I had waited so long to be at this stage and I was sure I could get through it, but the cold turkey had started to grind me down.

I knew Kitty had noticed the hole high up on the wall in the shop's kitchen.

I knew she knew.

I knew she knew I knew she knew.

We didn't mention it. We pretended not to notice it.

But I knew she knew.

I had been at work the day before, feeling blue and hating myself for it. The day had been quiet, a time to get on with pressing paperwork, but I just couldn't face it.

So I sat.

And sat.

And waited for customers but they must have had other things to do that day. Only a handful came in. It is a funny feeling waiting for someone to come into an empty shop. It is the thing you are longing for but when it happens, it feels as though they are disturbing you.

I had been having one of these days when I just wanted to eat. I had put the Back-in-Five sign up and bought the usual; 10p spicy bikers (four of), morning rolls (four of), two cans of Diet Coke, a round of Dairylea triangles and a packet of Skittles for afters.

Now, if you have never had a Dairylea and spicy biker roll, you really should. I ate all four rolls, trying to make them last but failing miserably. I thought about Lucy all those years ago nibbling at halved Wotsits. I wondered at how different people can be. Nick could sit watching telly with a Snickers on his lap, occasionally shaking the wrapper as if about to open it, then he'd place it back on his lap, fold his arms and focus again directly on the programme. I would be staring at the Snickers all the while telling myself that I would refuse a piece if he offered.

He never did. I always had to ask.

Amazed at my own gluttony I made a cup of tea and looked around for any forgotten packets of biscuits I could munch on. I reached up to a shelf littered with dusty cups and tea-making equipment and little boxes of 'miscellaneous-but-nevertheless-important' stuff. I trailed my fingertips into one of these boxes and felt a burn in my calves as I squeezed up onto my highest tippy-toes. I thought I heard the crinkle of a wrapper and made one last push. The whole shelf and not a little plaster fell down on top of me. My frustration and anger boiled over and I yanked the door to check that no customers had come into the shop. As it jolted open, it caught on the debris and banged into the side of my eye.

I let out a bellow.

I took deep breaths.

It wasn't enough.

I counted to ten.

It wasn't enough.

I picked up the sweeping brush and, lifting it over my head, slammed it into the top of the wall. The end went straight through the plaster board and stuck there.

It took me a good ten minutes of wrestling and climbing to get it out.

But to her credit, Kitty never mentioned it.

This tension with no release.
Coils.
Springs.
Winding.
Straining.
Waiting.
For what?

Present presents presence

We were unwrapping the mountains of Christmas presents down at the big ol' farmhouse. My Mum was delighted with the handmade sculptures I had made for her and my sister, and I in turn ooed and aaahd over our toiletries, books, pens and Babychams. After all the presents were naked of their twinkly paper, my Mum produced two more.

My sister received a beautiful elegant hand-carved giraffe. I unwrapped my gift slowly. It was a wooden hippo. It was so special.

'Aww, I'm afraid his wee ear's come off,' my Mum said, patting the hippo. It was the same size as a real warthog and was heavy.

'Did you bring these back with you?'

'Yes, don't you just love them?'

'Yes. They're amazing.' But I felt flat. My Mum had already given us so many gifts from Namibia and they had all been amazing – hand-crafted and unique. She had given away all her clothes, shoes and personal belongings to make space in her luggage. This carving was outstanding and I should have been emotional, grateful, at least happy, but I wasn't. I was flat. I could hardly smile. It was as if it wouldn't have mattered how wonderful the gift was because it wouldn't have moved me. I was quiet while Nadia admired her giraffe.

A little later when my Mum and I were alone in the kitchen,

she handed me a little tin with a teddy bear on it. She held her hands around mine round the tin.

'For you, from the Skeleton Coast.' Her eyes were searching mine as I opened the little box.

Sand.

It was the gift I didn't know I'd had been waiting for. I was holding the land that she had walked.

I felt like I was holding her ashes.

It's too fucking easy to sing the blues

Kitty and I were down at the farmhouse for a girly evening of drinking and poring over wedding magazines.

My sister's nuptials had been brought forward a year and nobody needed to ask why.

When Nadia had asked me to be the maid of honour I had cried and cried. My Mum was to give my sister away and it choked me to think of her walking her down the aisle. Kitty was also one of the bridesmaids along with every other female member of our family under the age of thirty.

It was to be an extravaganza.

Later, after we had had enough of looking at ladies in gowns and were tipsy from cider, my Mum mentioned the funny little toadstools she had seen in the paddock while walking the dogs.

'Really?' Kitty caught my eye. 'How many?'

'Oh, thousands,' came my Mum's bright-eyed reply. 'Come on. I'll show you.'

So we all piled out of the back of the house to the paddock. It was pitch dark and raining.

'We'll never see a thing in this.' I shielded my face from the rain with my arm.

'Hang on...open the gate for me.' My Mum disappeared from view leaving us to undo the chain and lift the soaking wooden gate over humps of grass. We heard her crank up the old Landrover she had painted white with non-drip gloss and watched it come bouncing through the gate. We all clambered on, Kitty on the roof, me on the bonnet and Nadia in the front. Off we went in search of magic mushrooms. Kitty and I screamed with the effort of hanging on, spread-eagled, while my Mum swerved about trying to bounce us off.

We parked in the middle of the field and watched as the ancient headlamps illuminated a sight of glory. Armies of tiny little helmets stretched as far as the eye could see.

We pulled plastic bags from our pockets and went to collect our bounty.

When we'd picked as many as we thought we needed, I jumped in the Landy beside my Mum as she ground and crunched it into gear.

'Mum?'

She turned to me, her eyes shining. She had been as exhilarated as we had been on our rain-soaked mission. 'This wedding is going to be huge.' I didn't need to voice my concern. She understood.

'I know. I know. But I have to do it.' At last the gear stick found a slot, albeit a wrong one, and the Landy lurched forward, bunny hopping out of the paddock. 'I had a dream the other night.' She waited until she had parked the truck before she continued. 'I dreamt that I was on my deathbed.'

'Oh Mum.' I reached over to her.

'Oh, stop your nonsense,' she batted my hand away and rolled her eyes. 'Everyone I'd ever known or ever met was coming to see me. There was a queue stretching out of the door and out onto the road and over the hill.'

'Like that Daniel O'Donnell DVD you gave Granny June?'

'Yes, exactly like that. Well, there was everyone, children, grannies, even that wee shopkeeper I used to get milk and dog food from on the way home, remember?'

'Mmm, hmm.'

'Everyone I've ever slept with, everyone I ever wanted to sleep with and even the love of my life was there.' She looked over with sad eyes. After my Dad had left for good she had had a love affair that had lasted for years but not for ever.

'Anyway, they all came to say goodbye. You and Nadia were either side of me and it started off fine. I was taking their condolences and thanking them but the trouble was that the more they came, the more I started to feel a bit better. I kept turning to you girls and telling you but you told me to shhh and to keep shaking hands. By the time the queue was getting near the end I was totally embarrassed. "Girls," I said when I had shaken the last hand, "I'm not dead yet. I'm going to disappoint them all. They've come all this way and I'm not dead."'

'But that's a good thing though, Mum,' I said to her, puzzled.

'No. No, it was dreadful.'

Nadia suddenly knocked on the window. 'Come on, guys. You've got some idiot tea to drink.' She was not impressed with our getting high even though she enjoyed collecting the means.

Everything became a bit soft and giggly after we had finished our mushroom brew. My Mum and Nadia retired for a hallucinogen-free night of sleep and left Kitty and me in a chuckling heap on the carpet. Thoughts of my Mum's mourners snaked their way around my imagination and it all felt very symbolic and important. I thought I should tell Kitty. It was one of the few times my Mum had discussed her inner thoughts and I wanted to share it now too. I felt very serious all of a sudden.

'Kitty?'

'Yeah?' She looked up from a little pile of tobacco and cigarette papers that she was attempting to fashion into something smokable. She must have seen my mood had changed because she put the half made joint down and picked up my hands. 'What is it, Laur?' She gave my hands a squeeze.

'Kitty?' I felt a sob form in my throat.

'What, Lauren?'

'My Mum's scared of snakes.'

'What?' But I couldn't answer her. I was in hysterics.

'What are you on about?'

I managed to catch a breath and wiped the tears off my cheeks. 'I've no idea!'

We both fell onto the carpet and shook with laughter until our bodies ached.

What the...

I was working in the shop and Kitty had popped round for the afternoon to keep me company. We were excited. We had arranged a big night in at her house. We'd got the wine, the music and perhaps a little something to give us a boost. It had been organised for about two weeks. Staying in; the new going out.

It was magic.

Just us girls chatting, giggling, exercising our genius and feeling sorry for the world at large who didn't, and couldn't, join in. The problem was, I was feeling strange, like I was exiting an escalator at the wrong time and had to hang onto the counter every now and then just to keep my balance.

'You know what? I think I might get a pregnancy test.'

Kitty looked at me, her head tilted. 'You're not late are you?'

'No idea. It's just, you know, tonight and everything.'

She shrugged and looked towards a customer who had just come in. I wasn't very concerned that I might be pregnant. I was so useless at predicting or knowing my cycle I would quite often take a test before a night out, just as a precaution. I could not handle the guilt of being drunk in charge of an embryo. Usually, after spending the eight pounds and watching the negative window appear, my period would arrive anyway.

The Device, The Devil & Me

I waited for a lull in trade and asked Kitty to cover for me. I sauntered up to the Kirkgate shopping centre and into Boots with a security guard on the door. I managed to find a test for £2.95 and strode quickly back to the shop. My two o'clock meeting was starting; sales agent Steve had arrived. I popped the test under the counter.

Steve. He was very young, cheeky, and sweet and, as it turned out, had his baby daughter in the car. He was very proud and asked to bring her in. I didn't really have much of a track record with babies, since most cried as soon as I feigned any sort of interest in them.

But Steve was so proud of his tiny girl that I went along with the enthusiasm for his sake and into the shop came a pretty little pink puffball. I braced myself for the scream as I said, 'Hello sweetie,' but nothing, not even a whimper. In fact the baby gave me a beautiful heart-melting smile! Kitty and I exchanged glances; she knew this was unusual. I became more and more aware of the little box under the counter. By the time Steve and his tot left I was desperate for a pee.

'Good luck,' Kitty cheered me on.

'Hang on, maybe I should call Nick to see if he wants me to wait and do it with him?' I very nearly forgot to ask because I was so sure of the result. I dialled his number.

'Hi, sweetheart, I've got a pregnancy test. Do you want me to wait and do it with you before I go out tonight?'

'Why, is it likely to be positive?'

'Well, no, but I have been feeling a bit weird recently and just wanted to rule it out.'

'Nah, you've probably got a cold or something.'

We said Bye and I went to the bathroom expecting my period to have come anyway as I could feel cramps. I opened the cheap cardboard box and assembled the kit as per the instructions. A little stick of what looked like blue litmus paper was fed through a little polystyrene doughnut which in turn would float in my urine in a miniature Chinese takeaway tub.

Digital First Response it was not.

I chuckled as I put the components together and filled the little pot. It said it could take up to three minutes for the stripes to show. I popped the floating stick into the liquid.

Immediately two big fat blue lines appeared.

And stayed.

And stayed.

I started shaking and wondered if maybe you had to wait for three minutes in case one of them went away. Three minutes, then five, then six. No, they weren't leaving. I checked the instructions again to make sure negative wasn't two lines. No, negative was one line.

The morning sickness hit me that instant. I retched, but to my own shock, it was an excited retch.

I poked my head out the bathroom door and scanned the shop for public. 'Kitty, it's positive.'

'Fuck off,' Kitty laughed.

'No, I'm serious. I'd better phone Nick.'

He was very quiet on the phone and sounded pale.

I shut the shop and Kitty drove me to Luca's for an ice cream (chocolate) and we sat in the car at the beach in disbelief.

The night out cancelled, Nick and I spent the evening sitting on our sofa not really knowing what to think. Responsibility, excitement and change hit us in waves. We had been together for nine years and decided that this was something to seal our unity.

*

I waited for the night terrors.

I lay in bed, wrapped myself up and braced myself for the onslaught.

I had always skirted around the idea of what would happen if I got pregnant. The worry over what I might produce made me shut out any desires of having my own children. I simply had to block it out. I lived day to day too scared to plan any future that might involve procreating.

So now it had happened. I was the owner of a tiny speck of life whose cells were doubling over and over as I lay still. Frantic motion.

Once again, I rallied the troops and built my defences and lay in wait.

*

I held my breath and kept my eyelids tightly shut.

It couldn't be morning, could it? I slowly opened my eyes to the sight of sun washing over the duvet. I had done it. I had slept the whole night through without one attack from a demon or even a single nightmare. For the very first time I felt truly awake. I felt refreshed.

As I lay with my hands gently on my tummy, I cautiously began to explore my feelings towards the baby. I began to imagine it growing safely inside me with all its little parts developing perfectly and in order. No sudden hideous images strobed themselves over my brain. No tiny red faced screaming devils marched past my eyes in nappies. Nothing that needed to be dramatically and harshly erased. There was only calm, soft contemplation.

It was amazing.

While I carried this child, I was immune. He couldn't touch me.

I let my excitement grow.

> *Look at my lovely food!*
>
> *Look at my yellow polystyrene box full of delicious slops! I'm not even checking over my shoulder as I plunge the plastic fork deep into the mound of cheese and coleslaw and butter and potato and salt, and salt, and salt. I load it until it threatens to snap under the weight of its filling and lift it to my mouth which tickles with guilt-free saliva.*
>
> *As I chew I am glorious.*
>
> *My body is ravenous and I absolutely stuff my face with utter joyous abandon.*
>
> *And after...*
>
> *I am happy.*
>
> *I am nourished.*

I arrived at the bar early.

My Mum was always early so I made extra sure to be there before her. I looked at the menu not knowing what to order, not sure if I felt like anything at all, even though I had a hunger

I had never experienced before. My stomach felt hollow and tight but my mouth was metallic and any smell seemed to send my temples wobbling with nausea. I found a seat and tried to ignore a cold sweat when some cigarette smoke wafted my way.

And there she was.

My Mum.

She stood in the doorway, wearing her full length black cashmere coat from Wallis. Her hair had grown back dark and curly, her trademark red lips smiled as she bounded over. She was on her way to a Namibian hike reunion and had decided to take the train. I had suggested we meet up before her connection to Glasgow. I had hardly been able to sleep the night before. She was carrying her Christian Dior vanity case with the red plastic manufacturer's tab still tucked through the combination lock, security against herself – if she couldn't lock it, there would be no danger of forgetting the code.

She ordered hot chocolate and I got a peppermint tea. It was still strange to me to see my Mum drinking something as innocuous as hot chocolate. All through my childhood she was strictly a caffeine and paracetamol woman. She had always had a mug of coffee in her hand, the rings on the inside of the cup revealing how many she had drunk and how long she had taken to drink them. A minimum of one every forty-five minutes. Until after one kidney infection too many, she cut out the caffeine and switched to hot water. Overnight.

It was dramatic. My Mum did nothing by halves.

So from then on she avoided caffeine at all costs.

I had witnessed the poisonous effects of the drug one night when my Mum, Nadia and I were getting ready for a meal out. My sister had discovered the delights of Pro-plus and we all took two washed down with a glass of pre-dinner Cava. Within half an hour my Mum's face flared up. Big red rough patches spread over her complexion.

'What's happening to you?' I had never seen anything like it before. She started shaking and her face swelled up even more. I touched her cheeks which were burning. I instantly thought cancer and felt my throat tighten over. Would it happen this quickly? Would it flare up within minutes? She had said that one day her breast felt normal and the next it was heavy and full with disease. I cancelled the dinner and checked my Mum's pulse. It was racing, hard.

'Mum, I'm calling an ambulance!' My sister grabbed the phone and began to dial. Then something dawned in my mind and I motioned her to put it down.

'Nadia?'

'What, Lauren? For God's sake!'

'Pass me that Pro-plus packet...' Fancy not looking on the back to check the ingredients! Fancy not deducing that it probably would have been caffeine! 'Damn it, Nads! We've missed out on a right swanky meal 'cos of this!'

I studied her clear skin now in the coffee bar. We chitchatted before the drinks arrived. I began to feel the nerves rising from my stomach in to my throat as I decided that now was the time.

'Mum, you do know that I'm not bulimic?' I saw the shock in her eyes.

'No, I would never use that word.' She was trembling and looked devastated.

'Because I'm not.'

'I would never betray your confidence. I know about your turmoil and what it can sometimes lead to, but I would never use that label.'

I was very, very ashamed of being called bulimic because in my mind I was not. There was more to it than that. Purging was just that: a way to relieve pressure in my brain without leaving marks. And of course, no one ever suspected because I wasn't even skinny.

Her pain was visible as she held onto my hands. I could feel her bones through her soft cold skin. She always groaned about having a man's shovel hands, but I only ever thought of them as hers. Strong and gentle.

'Anyway, none of that matters now.' I started smiling and she looked confused. I had said what I needed to say. It was time to move on.

'I'm going to have a baby.' I said.

She looked at me and hesitated, still trying to come to terms with the previous conversation. My news started to sink in.

'Lauren!' she was shaking and crying and laughing as she launched herself at me. We embraced for a long time as all our difficulties evaporated. I felt that in an instant I had grown from a troubled girl to a confident woman right there in my Mum's arms.

She ordered me the biggest chocolatiest fudge cake with ice cream and two spoons. We munched and chatted. Every now and then she stopped and stared straight into my eyes and whispered, 'I can't believe it. I can't believe it!'

We walked arm in arm to Waterstone's on Princes street, both bursting with excitement at our shared secret. She bought me the Miriam Stoppard's guide to pregnancy and child birth. I kept checking the time; I was worried she'd miss her train. I could tell she didn't want to go now. She wanted to spend the time with me instead, divulging womanly advice and love. But I knew this weekend was important for her. Namibia had changed her life and I didn't want her to miss this reunion with the people she had shared the experience with, something uniquely theirs. Too soon it was time for her train. I felt guilty that my news might overshadow her weekend. She told me not to be ridiculous. I walked her to the station.

She stood at the window clutching her little white case and didn't stop waving as the train pulled away.

I didn't stop smiling.

> *To hell with caution!*
> *I storm around my new space.*
> *I fly!*
> *I even seek Him out but He cannot be found!*
> *I am wild with joy.*
> *Full with it.*
> *You have made this happen.*
> *My little love.*

I lay on my back in the sunshine watching my belly writhe and quiver. There was a slow ocean inside me, vast and mysterious.

I was told you shouldn't lie flat on your back when you're pregnant but they didn't say why and anyway, I was invincible.

I had been out running round Arthur's Seat without a mobile. Nobody knew where I was. It was the first day of my maternity leave and I didn't have long to go. Some habits are hard to give up and I needed a naughty secret. I rubbed my bump and silently told it how we were partners in crime. I thought of my family and friends trying to contact me and it gave me a dark thrill.

I got up from my rest and continued on my way. I smiled gloriously at anyone I passed. I was so free. I almost hoped I would go into labour dramatically on the crags and would need to be air-lifted to hospital. My little daydream escalated as I hopped from rock to rock down a steep crumbling path.

A lady with stout walking boots and friendly face came towards me and stopped.

'Are you with someone?' she queried, concern in her voice.

'No, no, I'm just out enjoying this wonderful day. Actually I suppose I do have company.' I patted my belly. I was wearing a very tight t-shirt to emphasise my pregnant state.

'Yes, I gathered that, but you know, dear, it's maybe not that good an idea to be out alone on a hill in your condition.'

'You know, hardly anyone comments that I'm pregnant. It's taken nine months for people to realise I've not just been eating too many pies.'

The lady smiled. It was genuine but fleeting. I was high and my breathing was hard and excited.

'Does anyone know where you are, dear?' She repeated.

'Och, no. I'm fine, really I am. I just needed space, you know?' I was loving the attention and could tell she was impressed at how agile and strong I was. We were near the edge of a steep cliff and I was triumphant.

I had always wanted to fly.

I remembered the hours of running up and down the garden in my paper wings with my Dad watching. Those lovely big butterfly wings. I remembered how carefully he made them with his shaky hands and how beautiful I would feel as I cantered and bounced through the grass trying to take off.

My lungs were full of air and sunshine but as I exhaled, I noted concern in the lady's face.

'Listen, dear, could you do me a favour and head on down to the bottom now?'

'Why?' I was suddenly upset and ashamed.

'I just think that you should go and relax at the bottom.' She explained that she was a voluntary ranger and would escort me down if I liked. I was confused. Was I not an able, strong, healthy woman out conquering the day?

'It's fine, really. I'll be fine.'

'Good luck with the baby when it comes,' the lady said, smiling, while I wandered down the gravelly path subdued. I wasn't sure why, but I wanted to cry.

When I made it to the bottom I lay down in the green, green grass and tried to capture the magic I had felt up on the cliffs.

As I lifted up my t-shirt and let the sun blaze onto my tummy, the joy came flooding back.

All things bright and beautiful

It was later than I thought by the time my Mum and I got a lift home.

I was amazed we'd lasted so long. The wedding and reception had been just beautiful. The bridesmaids' dresses had quivered at the hem as we sobbed in the church.

While we sang 'All things bright and beautiful', I remembered my Mum gently singing the same words as she tucked me into bed as a little girl. I watched the tears splash on the ground, narrowly missing my bump and sandals. I stood with my head bowed, trying to force words out through my snivels, only blurting out the occasional 'moo' or 'made them all' much louder than expected. As usual my shakes of crying transformed into shakes of giggles as my bride-sister and Mum glanced round to locate the source of the intermittent bellowing.

My beautiful sister and her husband Ben were now Mr and Mrs Jones. My Mum and I had left them around midnight with all the guests still enjoying an almighty party.

I lay in bed making sure to log the day's events in my memory. I didn't want to miss anything out. As I went through the wedding minute by minute, guest by guest, I felt a warm trickle down the side of my chest. First the right, then the left. I was startled. I had no idea what was going on. I lifted the covers and looked down at my nightie.

My milk had started.

I felt like a little girl seeing blood on her pants for the first time.

I had crossed a threshold.

I got out of bed and went to my Mum's door. It was locked.

'Mum, Mum...' she came to the door. The telly was still on though I could tell she had been sleeping. 'Mum, I think I've started milking.' I started to cry. She took me in her arms; she knew how sensitive I was about things like this.

'Don't worry, darling, I can still squeeze milk out of my nipples after having you two. Look.' She began to undo her pyjamas and looked down.

Then stopped.

Our eyes met. I felt such sorrow. She must have relived that moment a thousand times.

'My doos...' We hugged again crying.

'Your don'ts.'

'That's right, my don'ts.'

We held each other for a long time, until the tears on our necks grew cold.

*

I was leaning over the banister wishing my Mum luck when I felt a trickle in my pants.

I tried to remain casual but she'd spotted it. A split second downward glance or a tiny intake of breath was all it had taken and she'd clocked it.

'What is it? What's wrong?' Her eyes turned from smile to panic in a flash.

'Nothing. Nothing! I mean it. Go on, you'll be late!' I smiled and urged her but she was already at the top of the stairs. 'Will you just go? I'm fine, honestly.' She was now holding my hand. 'Mum, go! You need this and it's on the NHS, so go!'

She had been referred by her forward-thinking country practice doctor for some reiki sessions and I was desperate for her to go and relax. She would never do it unless it was an official order and I knew she was looking forward to it. We were skeptical that it would actually heal her but the thought of her devoting time and silence to herself made me desperate for her to go. We had been discussing alternative therapies and holistic medicine just that morning and she had told me that she'd been reading Songbird. Eva Cassidy had explored many differing therapies and other ways to help her deal with her cancer. We talked of other women who had chosen to take up the fight. It was then, when I urged her to do the same, that my Mum had revealed the cruellest part of her disease to me.

'Lauren, those women all have something I don't; they all have partners and husbands to help guide them through their search. They have lovers to make them feel whole again in the long frightening nights. They have their rocks to fall on when their quest fails. I am my own rock. As I have always been. It's too hard. I have to choose my battles carefully.'

To my shame it was the first time I understood her loneliness. I had never given it any thought and now it was everywhere. She had once jokingly referred to 'never shagging again' on a wine-fuelled girls' night months earlier but we had quickly and nervously laughed it off. I distinctly remember taking what she had said and swiftly lifting the carpet and sweeping it away. To admit she would never again make love was the most heartbreaking of all. I was struck with the fullness of her void.

This beautiful and sensual woman would indeed never be made love to again.

'Please go and get the reiki, Mum, please.'

She eyed me and I held her gaze. 'All right, as long as you're sure.' She turned and started walking back down the stairs when Nadia came up behind me.

'What was all that about?'

I leant over and whispered in her ear, 'My pants are wet.'

'Mum, Mum!' she screeched and flew down the stairs. 'Lauren's waters have broken!'

What if?
What if I'm right?

'They've not! They've not, Mum.' She was already at the top of the stairs and was coming straight for me with panic plastered all over her face.

'Do you promise?'

'Yes, yes! It's just left over from the bath or something. Please, Mum, please, go to your reiki. You need it, you really do.'

Again, she walked down the stairs, eyeing me suspiciously every now and then. Eventually we heard the car roll off. My sister and I chatted excitedly about the prospect that I might be in labour but deep down I knew I wasn't.

Twenty minutes later we heard a car pull up outside. It was my Mum.

'I was too distracted. She told me to come home and be with you.'

I felt terrible. I felt like once again, I had sabotaged something precious. Taken away the focus. Impeded her recovery.

We waited for the rest of the afternoon for me to produce a baby, or at the very least, a labour pain.

Neither came.

What if something did get in even after all my precautions?

It hadn't even occurred to me that it might have been insensitive.

All I knew was that I wanted my Mum to be at the fitting of my nursing bra.

We stood together in the cubicle discussing what size of ginormous sling I would have to get when the assistant – sorry, expert fitter – swept back the curtains on their jangling poles.

'Now what can we do for you today? Maternity bra, is it?'

'Em, no, I'm here to be fitted for a nursing bra.'

The woman looked at my bump and said, with her hand placed on my forearm, 'We don't usually recommend getting fitted for a maternity bra until four weeks before the due date.'

I let my mouth drop open and looked from the woman to my Mum and back again.

'I'm due on Sunday!'

'Oh my goodness! I do apologise. We'd better get measuring then.'

I exposed my (apparently) small bump and my grey frayed maternity bra – the only one I had had throughout my entire pregnancy – £30 had made sure of that.

'Oh yes, I can see you properly now. Your clothes must have been covering you up.' She was embarrassed. She shouldn't have been; some people had thought I had just put on a bit of weight (aaarrrgghhh) and were surprised when I told them I was in the later stages of pregnancy. It seems odd to me that people feel completely free to give their opinion on the size and shape of your body and bump when you are pregnant.

'Oh you're neat,' was polite.

'Oh it's tiny. Are you sure there's a baby in there?' was disconcerting.

'My God, you're massive!' was devastating. *Am I?*

'You're not a woman with four weeks to go,' said my 'yoga for pregnant woman' teacher and pointed triumphantly to a lady sitting cross legged on the floor with a bump covering up her feet. '*That* is a woman with four weeks to go.' I had looked her straight in the eye and said, 'I defy anyone to say this baby won't be out in four weeks.' I was fed up and was determined my baby would be out on time. I felt a bit of pressure as both my sister and I had been three weeks early and so I was expected and expecting to produce my own likewise. Any day over that felt like a day over my actual date.

The cold tape wrapped around my ribs and under my massive boobs. It was expertly done in seconds.

'32G.'

'32G?!' The stuff of *FHM* magazine and Ann Summers' catalogues! My Mum could only stare at them and we started laughing.

I didn't really feel like laughing when the assistant returned with two 1950s style no-frills-no-under-wire cones that could have stuck straight through a bullet-proof vest let alone normal clothing. The idea that underwear in some cases can be used in the art of seduction had obviously been rejected at concept level. They had poppers at the strap so you could free the breast at a moment's notice without fear of losing that all important support. I tried one on, slipping my arms in and fastening the tiny eyelets behind my back, standing straight.

'No, no. You must lean forward and let your breasts fill the cups then scoop, lift and fasten.'

My Mum was in complete agreement though I'd never seen her scoop, lift and fasten. Thirteen years of wearing a bra and I'd been doing it wrong all along. Gawd only knows what damage I'd done.

My Mum bought me two of the enormous contraptions, one black and one white. I put on the white one and started to leave the shop with the strange sensation that only comes from seeing your own boobs elevated into your own field of vision.

'Excuse me?'

I turned round to see my filthy old bra dangling from the assistant's forefinger. 'You've forgotten to take this.' I asked her if she would be so kind as to deposit it in the bin. She smiled and obliged.

Cancel the football, darling

'You'd better cancel the football, sweetheart, we're having a baby today.' I bounced on the bed beside Nick as best I could with a massive belly that was threatening to contract again. It was Saturday; our baby was due on Sunday.

We'd got the nursing bra just in time.

'What? Oh, really?' Nick's face was rumpled with sleep and confusion. He fell back into his pillow and covered his head with the duvet.

'Darling, wake up, we're in labour!' I had been up since four o'clock timing the contractions and had decided to let Nick sleep so if it went on for a long time at least he would be rested and could gee me up if required. Not that I was anticipating a long labour, after all the timescale in the books is about 10–12 hours for a first baby and I had already done five. Yes, a nice little Saturday afternoon baby was just what I expected. I had the tens machine taped to my back and was quite enjoying the special feeling of swaying and breathing out the pain.

There was a snag.

I really, really needed the toilet but couldn't go. As the day went on and Nick declared how tiring it was having to time and write down the contractions, so my mood turned. I was well past my 12 hour perfect labour and the contractions were every six minutes or so. We decided to go to the hospital around midnight. Kitty took us in her car and waited to make sure we were okay.

The Device, The Devil & Me

'Just go,' I mouthed through the glass at triage and held the wall for support as my body was gripped by another contraction.

'I'll just make sure you're okay,' she mouthed back.

I swayed and rocked until we were called through. The midwife examined me and told me I was about one centimetre dilated and should go home and labour there until things intensified.

I couldn't believe it. One centimetre. You were supposed to do that in one hour not twenty.

I got back into Kitty's car with my tail between my legs and looked out of the window. I had never felt rage and disappointment like it. I couldn't speak to anyone and felt my spine grow spikes when Nick tried to comfort me. It was all I could do to dip my head to Kitty in thanks when she dropped us off outside our flat. We climbed the stairs and just as we got to the door Nick said, 'I wasn't convinced you were ready for hospital just yet.'

That was it; I had taken great care to hold the tiny inadequate lid on to my huge pot of emotion but now I let go of it.

'Fine, if I'm not in fucking labour, I won't be in fucking labour!' And with that, I ripped off the tens machine just as another wave of pain crashed on me. Only two of the electrodes came off leaving the other two to blast an almighty electric shock up one side of my back without the other two to counter it. It was agony but I was in such a fury that I tore off the other electrodes and stormed in through the door. Nick had been struggling as hard as he could to open it quickly. I threw myself onto the bed and tied myself up tightly in the duvet.

'If I'm not in labour I'm going to fucking sleep,' and I cried like a wretch as I tried to deny and block out any further contractions. Amazingly I felt the sweet relief of sleep pull me under.

> *It's dark and thick. I can see deep mist all around but I can't feel it. The blackness is so deep I can't imagine where it ends but it feels nice, comforting. I don't expect to feel this comfort. It feels so natural.*
>
> *I feel at peace.*
> *It feels like I have been here a long time.*
> *A very long time.*
> *Was I ever not here?*
> *I see something coming towards me. It is a person. A tiny person. It is a tiny old man. He has a wizened face. Tiny delicate features encased in lines. He could be Chinese. He is beautiful.*
>
> *'Oh, it's you,' I say. He doesn't reply. He takes my hand with the gentlest force and pulls me out.*

The tens machine had been replaced and I woke to find the beginning of a contraction taking hold. I curled up as tightly as I could and breathed and waited for it to wash away. I felt something tugging at my fingers.

> *His little hand leaves mine with the caress of a feather and I watch him disappear back into the mist.*
>
> *It doesn't frighten me to see him go for I know I'll see him again soon.*

All night I was guided through my labour. I woke up feeling refreshed and excited once again.

However, there was a problem.

I still couldn't go to the toilet. There was absolutely no way anything was coming out of that vicinity let alone a real human being albeit a tiny one. It was agony. All the straining was terrifying me and making me tense, the tenser I got, the tenser I got... I phoned the hospital.

'You can't self-administer a suppository whilst in labour.' *You stupid girl* her tone added. 'If indeed you are in labour.' The triage nurse sounded icy and very bored. I felt like just another, hysterical, first-time mother jumping to phone for advice at the slightest cramp. 'You will have to come in and be assessed.'

'But Sainsbury's is just up the road. I could just go to the pharmacy there.' The tone of the sigh which passed for a reply was of sheer disgust. I was shocked by the lack of empathy. This was my first baby; I felt special and wanted to be treated as such. I was hurt. 'Okay, we'll come back to the hospital.'

The midwife extracted a rubber-clad hand from me and said, 'Yes, you are quite bunged up, aren't you?'

Yup

'We'll have to get you upstairs for a suppository and you're still only one centimetre dilated so not what we would term "active labour".'

I couldn't believe it. Thirty-six hours of contractions and no further forward. It was hideous.

'We'll just pop this monitor on to see how baby's doing.' She strapped a tight belt around my bump and switched on the beeping heart machine. I felt another contraction coming on and squeezed Nick's hand. As the pain and tightening reached its peak, the little galloping heart monitor got slower and slower until it stopped.

I froze.

Oh my God.

The baby.

Its heart had stopped. My contraction eased off and I looked at the screen absolutely terrified. Slowly a beep returned, then another, then another until it had resumed a normal rhythm. I looked at Nick and began to breathe again. I couldn't believe it. My baby's heart was stopping every time I contracted. I would not contract again. It was as simple as that.

So I didn't.

I was in such shock that I told my body in total fury that it was not to do it again.

It didn't. I missed out four and the midwife who had been watching closely took me in a wheelchair up to the labour ward where everything started up again. They turned the heart monitor away from me and the volume down. I felt safe. The midwife was lovely.

'Right, let's make you more comfortable.'

I had to lie for twenty minutes while the suppository worked its magic.

'Oh my God what a relief!' Finally I pushed hard enough to splash several hard pellets out into the toilet. 'Nine and a half months of thinking we were pregnant and all we get is a bowlful of poops.'

The relief, though incredible, was short-lived as another contraction took hold. It was another four hours and severe unending pain with Nick staring into my eyes telling me how brilliant I was before the midwife gave us the news.

'I'm afraid you're still only one to two centimetres dilated.'

That was it.

'Nicholas, get me drugs!'

'But darling,' came the reply, 'remember the birth plan. Remember the yoga.'

'Fuck that!' I was in a terror frenzy, 'in fact, fuckit all, get me a gun and shoot me in the head, Nick.'

I was losing it but Nick took my face in his hands and managed to calm me down enough until the anaesthetist came.

Once the epidural took hold everything went brilliantly. The midwife broke my waters, my labour progressed and a mere six hours, two top ups of anaesthetic and a shot of ephedrine later, I was pushing.

'A boy, Nick! We've got a boy!'

The tiny little beautiful person lay on the bed between my legs. He was perfect. I recognised him immediately. This time it was my turn to take his tiny bewildered hand in mine. His wizened ageless face was so familiar.

'Oh,' I said looking into his blinking eyes, 'It's you.'

I had lain awake most of the night staring through the Perspex crib next to me.

It made so much sense.

Everything did. Every part of my life had led up to this moment. Nick lay behind me in the narrow hospital bed. His breath was the rhythm of sleep and his arms and legs clung around me with an equal measure of love and not wanting to fall off the edge.

My Mum had screamed with delight when I phoned and asked her to be the one to pick us up.

I wanted her to be the first.

We had forgotten our camera and were pleased when my Mum brought hers, albeit a Superdrug's disposable, and took our first exhausted images as a family. My sister was there too and we all cried together when we saw the tiny little person, small enough to be wrapped in a napkin with room to spare.

'I couldn't find the car park,' my Mum sniffed as we readied ourselves to leave. We began an endless snaking tour of the whole hospital and grounds before we finally found her car in an ambulance bay with a huge hospital sticker pasted on the side window warning of the evils of such parking.

The joy. I hoped she would never scrape it off.

We fussed and finally worked out the car seat.

My Mum drove us home.

We were home.

I was home.

The sippy cup

'What have they got you in a ward like this for?' I looked around the room which was too small for the number of patients.

I was livid.

If there was ever a reason to give up the fight, being put in this ward was it.

The hope was already gone from the eyes of the inhabitants of the other beds. In the bed nearest the door on the opposite side from my Mum's lay a wretched skeleton with yellowing ping-pong-ball eyes and patchy wisps of hair disfiguring her head. There was a baby blue Tupperware cup with a spout placed just out of her reach on the bedside table. Her eyes lolled around not looking at anything and momentarily settled on the cup before shifting again onwards towards their unreachable journey. I felt appalled at my reaction to this poor woman. I was disgusted by her. I felt devastated for my Mum that she was put in a ward where people were left to lie wishing the tea in front of them would come just a little closer and not be lukewarm with skin clinging to the inside of the plastic beaker.

'Jesus Christ, Mum, you're not dead yet. What's this all about?'

She grimaced in her tartan jammies with her lip lifted to expose angry teeth. She didn't say anything but I knew she felt the same as me. I wanted to ask the nurse if she had reached the end, was there nothing else they could do? Was this it?

My Mum had been admitted the previous day because she had had a rigour. We had been in her room chatting and listening to the muffled sounds of Nadia and Ben in the living room below.

'That cough sounds sore, Mum, do you want me to give you a back rub?'

'Ooo, yeah, go on.' She twisted herself round and lay face down on her bed. I began to feel my familiar way over her hard shoulders, not so big now but solid with tension. 'Mmmm,' she sighed as I massaged deeper and moved further down her back. It felt so comfortable to be rubbing her back. Throughout our years together we always used to rub each other's backs or brush each other's hair. The hours of rubbing and brushing. I remember being very small and creeping into her bed thinking I would be immediately banished as we weren't allowed to do that, but instead she cosied me into her and began to rub my back and neck round and round. It was luxurious and sensual nestled in under the warm bedding and feeling my mother's sleep washing over me.

I felt the rise and fall of her ribcage under my palms. Her breath had always been long and deep but tonight I felt a shudder at the end of her exhale. It was subtle at first but the more I concentrated, the longer it got. I thought maybe I imagined it and tried to fix my focus on the space between her shoulder blades. I pressed a bit harder and the shuddering intensified until she was shaking and coughing.

'Mum, are you all right?'

She couldn't answer me; she was choking and spluttering and flailing her arms trying to get up. I managed to roll her convulsing body over and pull her up to sitting but she fell forward, coughing and gagging into her hands. I passed her a cloth as the noise of the coughs was like a door slamming in an empty room. Hard and racked through everything. I started to panic. Her lungs gave out one last bellow through her throat and she spat something into the bit of material. She lifted it to her face and inspected it. It was a large yellow blob of mucus streaked with brown and red threads. She held it out to me. Her eyes were wild.

'It's the cancer, isn't it? It's everywhere.'

We called the hospital expecting an ambulance would be sent immediately but were told calmly to put my Mum in the car and bring her down to the out-of-hour's surgery. How serious did it have to be to be rushed to hospital? I felt disappointed for her as they didn't seem to take it seriously. My Mum had her own view on it though.

'They're surprised every time I show up. I think they think I should be dead already.' It was comments like this that made me wonder just exactly how much she knew about her condition and how much she chose to keep from us.

The cold-handed doctor placed his stethoscope on my Mum's back. I stood stiff and silent as my new baby stirred in his carrycot, and hoped he wouldn't wake. He was becoming quite the regular midnight-jaunt-to-the-hospital kinda baby and seemed to take it well.

'Yes, your chest is fairly congested down the lower left lung.'

'Is it the cancer?'

'No, I shouldn't have thought so, probably just a bit of fluid.' He was lying. I knew it. 'Better get you popped along to the hospital since you've had a rigour, a spiked fever, which could indicate an infection of sorts,' he smiled. He was an old friend of my Mum's from years before and I knew she had had a crush on him. I couldn't really gauge her reaction; her eyes were looking down to the floor.

So we dropped her at the hospital and waited while she got settled into her little one-bedded room with a window.

But at visiting time the next day, we were stunned to find a new patient in her bed.

Oh shit. Had she died?

'Heavens, no, dear. She's in ward 666, village of the damned, Dawn of the Dead and all that, just down the corridor.'

And that's where she was.

'Let's shut the curtains.' I pulled them tight around us to shut out the misery beyond. It did make a difference and we began to chat like normal.

'Are you excited about the move, Mum?'

Throughout the past few weeks she had been using her life insurance money to buy a new house with a granny flat for her, Nadia and Ben to live in. She had joked that it was the last thing she would do and when she finally lay down in her new bed in her new room in her new house, that would be it, she would lay down her head and die. She had joked.

I knew she meant it.

'Yes.' Her eyes regained a bit of their old sparkle and I could sense a triumph in her. It had been a battle but she had won it. She had pleaded her case to get the insurance money, the cancer had to be terminal or there would be no payout, not while she was still alive anyway. She had had to tell them over the phone and in letters that, yes, she was indeed dying and wouldn't be around much longer, so, can I get my money now? They had believed her. I don't know what medical documents or evidence she had had to include but it must have been convincing as the company had deposited the money in her account on the very day she needed it for the new house. In her usual 'I will do this' style she had gone ahead and placed an offer on the house, got it, and secured a mortgage for the balance before she had even found out if her claim would come through.

'Of course it will,' she had told me during one of my concerned chats. 'I'm fucking dying, aren't I?'

'I don't think I can handle the move though. I don't want to be there for that.' She just didn't have the energy. She had already started to sort out her belongings and pack but the little she had done had left her exhausted.

'We'll take care of it, Mum, don't worry.'

'Hello-oo?' We were interrupted by a figure flittering about on the other side of the curtain obviously trying to find the entrance. I made a face at my Mum and leaned over and pulled back the edge.

'Oh, silly me!' A friendly-looking woman with big speckly black hair smiled in at us. 'I'm Anne-Marie from palliative care, just wondering if you would like to discuss your treatment and medication.'

'Palliative care?' I was frightened. Palliative care meant there was no hope at all. I stared at my Mum and felt like I was accusing her of something. 'It's not time for that yet. Is it?' I looked from my Mum to Anne-Marie who looked uncomfortable.

'There's no reason to worry,' she told me. 'Palliative care is nothing sinister. It is merely the term we use for controlling symptoms and making patients in your mother's circumstances comfortable.' Sounded like the language of death to me. 'It includes all kinds of therapies and medicine, for example, we can offer not only physical relief but spiritual relaxation as well.' Sounded exactly like the language of death to me. I sat silent staring at the words being formed in this woman's mouth. They floated about and I started to hallucinate that I could reach out and catch them, maybe put them safely in my pocket before they reached my Mum. 'I can come back later if it would be better.'

'Yes, I think that would be better.'

'I'll leave this leaflet for you to have a look at. I'm in on Tuesdays and Thursdays.' She smiled really kindly and I felt sorry that I'd been so hard and negative with her. 'It really isn't what you're imagining,' she looked straight at me. 'We just want your Mum to be as comfortable as possible.' She gave each of us another smile and pulled the curtain back into place.

'You don't need palliative care do you, Mummy?'

'Naw, don't be daft.' She rested her head away from me on her pillow.

'I'm just going to get something from the canteen; I'll bring you some Lucozade.'

It's so easy.
This place is so large, so spacious.
So free.
How did I ever fill it so?
Correction, how did we ever fill it so?

Living in this space without battle is so easy, so easy and pure.

I can't believe how many years I have lived without it.

I can breathe.

I am not even checking over my shoulder for this spell to break.

I am no longer walking on a web of shattering crystals.
I am on solid ground.
Even life with death is easy.
Even life with pain is easy.
Even life with loss is easy.
As long as I have this space.
It is all so easy.

Ladybird, ladybird fly away home, your house is on fire, your children are gone

I had almost doubled in size and yet I was still trying to squeeze into the size 12 pure wool maroon jacket from Wallis. I just managed it and the buttons strained together threatening to split as I turned to face my sister.

'Whaddya think?' I twirled and winked and she handed me the open bottle of Cava. I took a swig and leaned over, trying not to snort the foaming bubbles out of my nose.

'Aye, you're gorgeous! Check me out!' Nadia was also crammed into clothes that were getting tighter by the layer.

We were in my Mum's bedroom going through her wardrobe. We'd had to get drunk to do it. I kept my word and while she was still in hospital Nadia and I started packing up her belongings. Archie lay contented and fast asleep in the spare room that my Mum had transformed into a nursery the week I'd told her I was pregnant. Under the many garments I was wearing was a portable baby monitor. I knew we wouldn't need it though; Archie had slept through the night since we brought him home from the hospital. My sister and I would be free to complete our task.

'Just chuck the whole lot out,' my Mum had said when we had been to see her earlier that day. 'Chuck the whole bastard lot.'

The Device, The Devil & Me

So Nadia and I had had to finish a bottle of wine at the kitchen table before we were ready to venture upstairs.

'Right, you have to see how many things you can get on at once, okay?'

'What's the prize?'

'Looking goo-ood...'

We'd pulled on trousers and tops, shirts, jumpers, knickers and dresses. Now it was time for the jackets. I was hot and it was almost impossible to bend my arm at the elbow. I had to crane my lips towards the neck of the bottle. The action made me topple and laugh all over again and we decided we probably had enough clothes on to go on down to the fire.

We had already been burning rubbish and garden waste in the late afternoon; old bits of broken furniture had been pulled out of the skip we had hired and filled in a matter of hours, and burned to make way for more. My Mum wanted to travel light to the new home and we took her words literally. We wanted to do something for her. We wanted everything to be gone for her coming home so she wouldn't have to deal with the task of getting rid of her own memories. She was strong, but perhaps not that strong. Her quiet compliance during visiting hour had given us the permission we needed and we went to the task with gusto as soon as we got back. We had sorted out everything in all the other rooms of the house, organising, boxing, skipping and burning. We had been silently ignoring the upstairs bedroom which held everything of her. Clothes, bed, make-up, scent. Now that we were drunk and had begun, there was no stopping.

We made our way stiff and wobbling down the stairs, deliberately bumping into each other, trying to knock each other over. The fire was still going and we did the strip tease dance while we tugged items off. We had to help pull each other out of the perfectly good, clean clothes before we flung them on the fire. I thought the fire would be smothered as the thick garments flopped over the flames and covered them completely. For a few seconds everything went dark and muffled and I was filled with sudden regret. I looked at Nadia who quickly changed her sadness to smiles when she caught my gaze. We couldn't cry.

Not yet.

Just in time the flames licked up and over the jacket and my sister and I exhaled. We pulled the rest of the clothes off and one by one threw them on to the pyre, every garment giving us a memory of our Mum.

That was the coat she bought the day I'd failed my driving test. She'd let me skip school and we went spending to make me feel better. There's the shirt she wore on that date with...Oh no, those are the trousers she wore to Namibia.

I was glad when Nadia spoke. 'Come on, let's get some more.' Before we went back upstairs we threw some more bits of broken table from the skip on the fire.

We were on our ninth item each when Nadia found it.

'I didn't think she'd kept any of these.' Her eyes glazed with the beginnings of tears and she snapped them back with a sniff.

My sister held out her arm and dangling from her hand, pinched delicately between her thumb and finger, was a bra. It had been my Mum's favourite. Lacy, black, underwired, feminine. It was like reading someone's diary.

It was awkward.
It felt wrong.
But we couldn't cry.
Not yet.
I took another swig of Cava.

'Fuckit. Put it on,' I said, taking it from her and pulling it up over her blanketed arms and body. I pressed my foot into her back and pulled the straps together like something out of *Little Women*, and fastened the hooks together over the jumpers and coats.

It burned so quickly. It melted and turned to fiery lace before we could get used to the idea that we had even thrown it on.

And like that
It was gone.
Now we cried.

Familiarity breeds contempt

The hospital.

The familiar bed, the familiar room, the familiar window, the familiar view.

It's amazing how quickly things become familiar, comfortable. Even my Mum's frail thin body wearing pyjamas in the daytime was now familiar.

Mostly the cancer just took things away but sometimes there were additions. Today it was little black crosses tattooed onto her skin: markers for the radiotherapy to find the precise location of the tumour now striding into her brain. I was used to them already. Familiar.

My Mum smiled her now clenched familiar smile as we played with the baby on the snack-strewn hospital bed. Crisps and juice had been consumed. Sometimes she had no appetite but today we had had orders to bring snacks. Crisps, chocolates, sweets. She had opened every packet and had just a taste of each but nothing had hit the spot. I could sense an atmosphere building and tried desperately to keep things light, shifting focus onto the gurgling baby. I could tell my sister felt the shift too as she sat stiff in her chair with a cushion held tight on her lap: a sure sign she was uncomfortable.

'Oh, Laur, he's so gorgeous,' Nadia said, quickly glancing at my Mum whose smile had turned to a grimace and whose eyes had darkened. I was suddenly sad and scared. Nadia started to say something about her friend who was trying to get into art college.

'Maybe you'll be a famous artist one day,' she said to me with a wink.

My Mum looked over and her face turned to a sneer. 'No, she won't, she's got no drive or ambition.'

I felt like the Devil had just severed my spine at the base of my skull and my soul had dropped out to the floor. Out of the corner of my eye I could see the shock on my sister's face.

I was changing Archie's nappy and threw myself into the task as if I hadn't heard. 'Where's Mummy's big boy, where's my baby?' I tickled him with all my concentration. I couldn't look at anyone yet. The significance of that statement was immense. I had never once in my life heard anything other than encouragement from my Mum. After all these years of investment and nurturing from her, was I really a disappointment? I felt like part of me had crumpled. She always told me I'd win an Oscar one day and had made me promise that she would be my guest. She truly believed that one day I would be on that stage, in that position. She had made me believe it too, but somewhere deep down I kept my Devil, who in turn kept me down. I was just devastated that she would go to her grave believing I wasn't the person she thought I was.

From anyone else in the world it could have been dismissed as a throw-away comment, but from my precious Mum who was an eternal morale booster, it was a blow. I tried to rationalise it as pure frustration on her part and that of course she didn't really mean it. Perhaps the cancer in her brain had altered its chemistry. It was awful. She was to die before I could prove anything to her. She'd always said it didn't matter. She loved me and supported me no matter what I did.

Isn't it strange how twenty-six years of absolute bolstering and support can be shattered by one tiny sentence? I was disgusted with myself for letting this be so. I abhorred taking on her pain as my own. But most of all I was embarrassed.

Embarrassed at letting her down.

This tone, this voice, this person was something I could never let become familiar. No, some things cannot become familiar. You cannot let them.

Later, I walked through the car park with Nadia, pushing my sleeping Archie in the buggy.

She mentioned it first.

'I can't believe she said that. I'm absolutely gutted for you.' Her eyes showed true sympathy.

'Do you think she meant it?' I asked.

The shock on her face was jolting.

'No! God, no, Laur! She's just devastated that she's going to die and miss all our lives. She's so, so proud of you. Look at your little boy! She adores you!'

'I know, Nadia,' I said wanting to cry, 'but I just can't bear the thought of being a disappointment to her.'

'You're not, she's just frustrated.' Nadia hugged me and we both sobbed. She said not to take any notice because my Mum was probably turning daft anyway with the cancer in her brain and all.

I hang my head and wait again.
   Something has stung me but I can't tell what.
   It doesn't feel like Him but I can sense him.
   I can sense him lying in wait.
   Outside the sphere.
   Please don't come back.
   Please.

Merry Christmas everyone

It didn't feel right.

Granny June, Nadia, Ben, Nick and I sat around the old pine table filling our bellies with Christmas delights. Archie slept in the living room where my Mum sat on the sofa with a tray of trimmings going cold on her lap. She had said she wanted to be alone and we had reluctantly left her before she'd had to insist.

We were noisy. Crackers and booze. Jokes and raucous laughing.

Anything to drown out the silence coming from where my Mum and my baby were. Sometimes we slipped into conversations and anecdotes that distracted us. But only for a minute. As soon as we relaxed we'd remember and stiffen again. Guilty eyes would pause to search the door before quickly rejoining the strained joviality.

Ben had cooked a delicious lunch and we had really enjoyed it, eating way more than we should have and taking far longer than we usually would. Eventually all the plates had been scraped and put in the dishwasher. The two men left the pots to soak which were swiftly scoured by Granny June.

There was nothing left to do but creep slowly through to the living room.

I looked quietly round the door to see my Mum staring blankly through the baby's carrycot, her dinner untouched on the tray. She had the eerie tension of someone sleepwalking.

I thought for a second she was actually asleep but she stirred and noticed me in the doorway. She flicked a switch and turned on her smile. The muscular effort in her face was incredible.

Then it was gone.

She adjusted the legs of her glasses under her woolly hat, a motion that was fast becoming a trade mark of her weariness, and lay back. I took this as my prompt to remove her tray.

She didn't say Thank you.

There was nothing left to do in the kitchen; the food had been eaten, the drink had been drunk and, thanks to Granny June, the dishes had been done. There was nothing left but to venture through to the living room and open the presents. We all hesitated. It is strange to buy gifts for someone you know is going to die. What can you buy? What can you buy that will be of use, or of comfort? I eyed the tiny package I had so carefully wrapped for my Mum. I had gone to an antique jewellery shop and found a miniature silver duck. It was beautiful and the detailing was perfect. I was sure that she would love it. Well, I was fairly sure she would love it. It came in a green suede pouch and reeked of quality. It was the first expensive thing I had ever bought for my Mum.

I handed her the package and she placed it on her lap. She motioned for me to get on with opening some of the gifts stacked up in a huge pile under the tree. As we all swapped presents I occasionally looked over to see what my Mum thought of her duck, but it remained unopened. Just like one of Nick's Snickers bars.

'I think I'll go to bed,' she said suddenly and abruptly. I was kneeling beside Archie opening his mountain of presents while he just kicked out a leg occasionally. I watched as Ben pulled her out of the sofa slowly and painfully.

'Do you want me to come up with you?' I asked, hoping that she would say no. Of course she said no.

'I'm fine, finish opening your presents.'

'Okay, Mum. I'll check on you later. Merry Christmas.' I got up and kissed her cheek. She seemed too frail to hug today.

'Merry Christmas, everyone. Thanks for the presents.' She shuffled out of the room on Ben's arm, leaving the little pile of gifts unopened on the sofa.

> *I retreat into my space.*
> *How could it have been so full before?*
> *How could it have been so crammed?*
> *I roll around in it like a lady in a flowery field eating a Flake.*
> *It is magical.*
> *There is no guilt here.*
> *There is no anger or hate.*
> *Why not?*
> *Where has it gone?*
> *Shhh...*

My Mum was swigging back liquid morphine like a Deadwood cowboy.

She was rubbing the little silver duck I had given her between finger and thumb though her eyes, wild and drugged, did not see it.

'Do you know, Christmas has always been my favourite time,' she paused then looked at me.

'I know you love Christmas! You always make it so special for us.' She looked so sad.

'I wanted it to be special for you; I wanted you to have the magic.' She had. And she did. Around my Mum, Christmas was always magical.

'What was it like for you?' I asked her while she took another swig. I had noticed she opened up the same way on liquid morphine as she used to on alcohol. The difference was, whilst drunk, it was the men in her life that bore the brunt of her rantings but on Oramorph her mind delved further into her past, my childhood. I had never really thought about how hard it must have been for her to keep smiling while her family fell apart. The joy of sharing Archie's first christmas with Nick was amazing – I could never imagine him not being there.

I visualised my Mum wrapping presents and playing Santa all alone. It made me remember my worst Christmas.

It was the night before Christmas Eve and my Mum and Dad had had a huge and violent fight. My Mum had grabbed Nadia and me, wrapped in jammies and duvets, and fled to Granny June's. I remembered the excitement. Granny June's house was always warm and welcoming. Soon we managed to forget about why we were there and were able to concentrate on Christmas and Santa. On Christmas morning we had a wonderful time without the tension that always hung between my Mum and Dad. I didn't get the Spirograph I had asked for but I managed to content myself with other presents.

Then my Mum announced that it was time we went to see my Dad back at home.

Nadia refused to come. I couldn't. I wished I had it in me to say, 'No. I don't want to come.' But I didn't. So I sat silent in the car. When we got home, I sat quietly on the floor. I knelt near the window with my bottom on the ground and my feet turned out. I knew it was bad for my knees – we had been told in gymnastics to never *ever* sit that way but I didn't care. I could feel pressure on my hips and the insides of my knees pressed painfully into the floor. I leaned forward slightly to increase the sensation. It was the first time I had done something knowing that I might physically damage myself in some way and it seemed to relieve some tension. For a fleeting moment I felt soothed. My Mum sat behind me on the edge of the sofa and my Dad sat weeping by the wood burning stove. I had my back to them both.

The box lay wrapped in thin Christmas paper over my thighs. I knew exactly what it was but my desire to unwrap it vanished.

I didn't want a Spirograph any more. The hours I had spent wishing and aching for one now made me feel sick and stupid.

'Go on, open it,' my Dad pleaded. I caught an excitement in his teary eyes at how he'd done so well and got me exactly what I wanted. I started to cry as I tore open the paper as slowly as I could.

Eventually there was no more Christmas paper left to hide in and I had to open the box.

I assembled the pieces of the Spirograph and pushed the round headed pins into the grid paper and cardboard. The pins were soft and kept bending, the plastic guide wasn't firmly held in place and the cogs, wheels and pencil wobbled about the page without proper control just making scribbles.

I was so disappointed.

'Thanks, Daddy, it's just what I wanted.'
I was desperate to go back to Granny June's.

Now I sat all grown up watching my Mum absently playing with the useless present I had given her knowing that we had just shared our last Christmas together.

'I'm sorry I got you that stupid fucking present.'

Her face remained expressionless. She took another swig of her Oramorph and was about to say something but stopped.

Dread poured through me. She would be gone soon.

I grabbed her arms and let my body flop pathetically into her lap. I sobbed and cried and felt awful for doing it.

'Come on, don't be daft, it's all right.' She cradled my head and stroked my hair. How would I cope without this strength?

Even at her weakest she was stronger than me.

I knock.
  I wait.
  There is no answer.
  I knock once more just to make sure.
  I leave.
  Happy.

The countdown begins

I looked into the sitting room, now her sick room. She lay on the sofa, all pale and tiny. She seemed to take up hardly any space any more. Every breath made her shake. Pain streaked through her eyes as her body racked forward with a hard gargling cough. She lay back again and paused for the sofa to take her weight before the skin settled back over her stark brow.

I knocked gently and crept in, the baby in his carry seat.

'Hi Mum.'

'Hiya sweetheart, where's my boy?' I lifted Archie out of his chair and held him up to her. She reached out with her frail arms and asked me to put him on her knee. A flicker of light sparkled in her large broken eyes. She tried to smile.

'He's so beautiful, my beautiful boy.' The words barely made it to my ears.

'How are you feeling?'

'Fine,' she said.

I took Archie back and laid him in his seat. He would sleep now.

I couldn't bear the fact that she couldn't walk any more. Worse than that, I couldn't bear the fact that she stared vacantly at the TV all day long watching rubbish. I brought through her little CD player and put on a Ben E King and the Drifters album. I stood behind the sofa and brushed her short hair. Once again it fell away with every stroke. I abandoned the brush and started massaging her head instead. As I rubbed and kneaded at her scalp and follicles, what was left of her patchy hair fell out into my hands and rained onto the floor around my feet.

Her silence was huge.

At last she turned her head slightly towards me. I could see the effort it took.

'Has it all come out?' she asked in a throaty whisper.

'Yes.' I kissed her on her bald head and started kneading her shoulders. Hunched now, sloping and skinny.

When I got home that evening, I wept and wept into Nick's lap. I let it all out onto his strong thighs as he stroked my hair.

I awoke with renewed hope. It was a crisp frosty day, the kind of day that filled me with an excited buzz. I knew my Mum wasn't going to get better but it was okay.

Then the phone rang.

'This is it, Laur, she's going into hospital. The ambulance is on its way.' Nadia's voice was calm yet frantic. It was an odd combination but one I utterly understood.

I knew this would be the last time. I tore about the house trying to gather the baby's things. Nick took the day off work and tried to keep me calm while I threw everything into the car. It was snowing on the drive down but my one thought, all the way, was that I had to be with her in the ambulance. The journey took for ever. I thought I had my foot to the floor but we were endlessly on the same road.

'Try to calm down,' Nick kept saying, but panic was engulfing me.

'We'll never make it, we'll never make it. Come on, come on.' My jaws were clenched and aching, my spine rigid and I leant forward in the driving seat as I flew round corners and over bumps. My eyes took in every tree, bush, corner, fence, building, sign, cloud, all in slow motion.

We pulled into the drive and saw the ambulance still there, back doors open, empty inside. The gravel spun under the tyres with the force of the brakes. I flew out of the car and ran to the open front door. Nadia ran straight into me. We embraced and nodded at each other.

'Are you going in the ambulance?' she asked me.

'Yes.'

She looked relieved.

'Are you?'

Tears brimmed in her eyes and she shook her head.

'I can't, I can't. I just can't.'

She had been my Mum's carer for the past year; she had done more than enough. It was my turn to offer what I could.

'I'll do this, Nads.' I held her shoulders. 'Don't worry.'

Nadia wandered off into the trees at the bottom of the garden. I could see guilt and grief weighing on her. I felt like I was in a trance as I walked in to where my Mum was. Everything felt dreamlike. Two paramedics stood either end of the sofa smiling at my Mum, telling her she'd be comfortable soon. She sat with her head bent over, pyjamas still on. Blue tartan. And her woolly hat which bulged at the ears where her glasses slotted in.

For a moment I watched the scene from the door like a film. One of the paramedics noticed me and tapped my Mum on the shoulder.

'Joyce, your daughter's here.' She must have told them I was coming. Her brow looked up first, followed by her glasses then her eyes. It was so slow. She couldn't smile.

'I need to get ready.' She looked back down again.

One of the paramedics leaned in to my Mum.

'We'll just be outside, Joyce. Take your time.' They left us alone together.

My Mum's beige combat trousers and jumper lay folded on the arm of the sofa, a chesterfield she'd recovered and restored. I pushed my arms in under hers and eased her to a bowed standing position. She pulled down her pyjama bottoms and flopped back onto the sofa naked from the waist down. I was shocked. I quickly found her pants and pulled them up over her wasted legs. I had to haul her up again so she could pull them over her hips. I got the trousers and did the same with those. She lay back on the sofa and brought her wrist to her brow. Eyes closed.

She was simply exhausted.

With everything.

When she had regained some energy from the effort, I helped her to lean forward so that she could unbutton her pyjama top. She had been so private about her body since the operation and I wasn't prepared for the way she now abandoned this privacy. She started from the bottom button and worked painfully slowly up, pausing between each hole. It was like watching a slow motion dream or nightmare. When she finally got to the top button she let the two halves fall open and I eased it off her shoulders. She was stark and exposed but she didn't have the energy to care.

'Do you want your bra on?' I spoke softly and she motioned with her hand, keeping her gaze on her knees, towards the black satin strapless bra which gave her definition over her scars.

I looked at the scars. I had not seen them since the hospital. Then they had looked new and even had an elegance to them; her breasts and cancer had been taken away but the red brandings left in their wake had meant hope. Now they were malevolent scars of defeat.

They were dark.

I held up the garment that was like a double eye patch and reached around her back to fasten it. She seemed to be in a trance, letting me deal with her body as if it no longer belonged to her. I didn't even think about what she was thinking. I didn't even think about what I was thinking. It was a strange silent serenity. I pulled her beige crocheted jumper over her head and eased her arms in.

Once she was dressed with her hat and glasses replaced, she lifted her head and said simply, 'It's time.'

I waited outside as the ambulance crew strapped her into the stretcher with a tartan blanket tucked in under the belt. As they took her into the vehicle I caught sight of my sister breaking down in her husband's arms. She looked at me with grieving wet eyes and told me how awful she felt at not going in the ambulance with my Mum. We hugged and hugged until I was called in.

Just before we left, my Mum opened her eyes and looked at me directly. 'This is it. I won't be back.'

I held onto her hand. There was an oxygen saturation

monitor attached her left middle finger that read ninety-two percent.

'That's good news, isn't it?' I looked up at the paramedic.

'Actually, no, we'll just pop this mask on to bring it up a bit.' She slid the elastic expertly over my Mum's head with outspread fingers without disturbing her hat or glasses.

The nurse at the hospital assured us my mother was in capable hands.

'Don't you worry,' she said as she showed us to the pink-walled homely room. 'We are professionals. We deal with this all the time. Use us how you need to. If you want a hug, we'll open our arms, if you want to scream and shout we'll listen, because we are angry too at what you are going through. We are sad and angry at what's happening to your Mum, just a young woman. Believe me, we understand and we will do everything we can to make her comfortable.'

My Mum was already lying on her bed, smiling at the nurse. I noticed that whenever the nurse had her back turned, involved in a sorting-the-room-out-and-arranging-the-chairs task, my Mum's smile faded. She was still doing it even now, on her death bed. She was trying to make the nurse feel better about the situation. The smile was like she was standing to attention and I wanted her to stop. I sat on a comfy slidey leather chair and lifted up my top to feed Archie. For a while, the nurse focused her attention on making me more comfortable, asking if I needed a drink or some food to help with the breastfeeding. At first I lapped it up. It was nice to be important and what could be more important than feeding a baby.

I stand with the mirror before me.
I look up, eyes down.
I open them.
Doorways are all around me.
They are unlocked and welcoming.
I choose one.
I reach out.
I look behind me just to check.
Nothing.
I turn back with my hand ready to close around the handle.
The doors are gone.

The next morning at the hospital we were called in for a meeting with the doctor.

We sat in a circle on mismatched worn chairs in the family room. I looked at Ben with his arms tight around my sister. My sister looked at Nick with his arms tight around me. My Mum would have loved to see us like this – her girls with their men. Though perhaps under different circumstances. Ceramic birds and flowers sat gaudy and cracked on lace clad book cabinets. This room was used as a respite room for families on vigil. They were trying to create a homely feel. Whose home, I do not know, but they had made the effort. Woodchip and walls and fire exit procedures rained down on us as we waited for the doctor to speak.

'Nurse Davies and I had a chat with your Mum today.' Nadia and I looked at each other.

A chat?

How was that possible? She had been lying in an intense stupor the whole time we had sat at her bedside, untangling her sheets, checking the urine bag. Getting up to the toilet was an ordeal for her so she had been catheterised during the night. We had already straightened out a kink in the toffee coloured tubes, dark brown through dehydration.

She certainly was incapable of having any sort of conversation with us.

'She was extremely lucid at the time and has been quite direct in her wishes,' he paused and made brief, awkward eye contact. 'She is no longer capable of swallowing medicine and has requested a syringe driver.' A few months ago I had never even heard of a syringe driver. It was all too big a part of my vocabulary now.

We knew what it meant.

The syringe driver would administer enough diamorphine intramuscularly to take away the pain and send my Mum unconscious. Not enough to kill her outright; *that* would be murder. She was refusing all other treatment. Her own body would do the killing. Deprived of fluid, medicine and nourishment it would slowly starve and dehydrate her to the point of complete organ failure. She had made her wishes clear.

'How long will it take?' I asked the doctor, daring him to give me a straight answer.

'We need you to prepare yourselves for a long wait. The body can sometimes take up to two weeks to die.'

Two weeks? I couldn't believe it. If she had made the decision to die, it would have to be now. This was a cruel blow. I didn't want to think of her in limbo for another night, let alone fourteen.

'When are you going to do it?' My voice started to quiver and I swallowed hard.

'As soon as possible. We just have to set up the equipment.'

I panicked. 'Let us say goodbye first!'

'Of course,' said Nurse Davies, 'but she gets very distressed when you cry, so try not to.'

My.

God.

my

god

We went back to the room. My Mum lay with her eyes forced closed, like a child feigning sleep or hiding. I could tell that if she could have closed her ears over she would have done that too. She had wound herself into a cocoon. She did not want to be reached by us any more.

It was hard to take.

It was hard to accept that the last conversation she had had was with a doctor, giving him permission to end her life, not saying goodbye to us. We had had plenty of dress rehearsals over the past months, but nothing like this moment.

She was lying in a semi-foetal pose with her arm tight over her chest. Everything was defensive. Her body looked scared. I know she wasn't afraid of dying but I knew it was excruciating for her to be leaving.

I placed my hands on her feet and massaged them. They felt so small, these mighty feet. When I was a wee girl, I would do operations on her them which would involve bathing them in the washing-up bowl with Fairy Liquid then sprinkling entire pots of talcum powder on them and scraping it off again. She would often fall asleep during my attentions which I didn't mind because it meant I could be the nurse for longer. Holding my breath if she stirred, scared she would get up and find something pressing to do.

Now, I sat massaging her feet, holding my breath, waiting for her to stir, knowing there was only one pressing thing for her at that moment. I hoped that they hadn't told her it could take up to a fortnight.

For years she had been trying to get me to resume my childhood care of her feet, but they had been over-used and were tough and cracked and the nails were hard and yellow. She would call them her scabby feet and wriggle and rub them on us. We would squeal and run away from them, repulsed. In the time she had been in this hospital, I had started taking care of them again. Massaging and rubbing. I could see the relief it brought even though she would protest and say they were scabby.

I told her I loved her scabby feet.

*

I sleep, I pray

I pray it will be quick.
I pray you will be welcomed.
I pray you will rejoice.
I pray you will dance.
I pray you will be free.
I pray I will be there, waving you off.

*

Gone
    I'd missed it.

I'd languished in the illusion that I still had time. Still had time to go home. Still had time to sleep. Still had time to wake up slowly, clean my teeth, take a bath. I even believed I had time to shave my legs.

The doctor had said we should go home for some rest. So Nick and I did. And we'd missed it.

As we raced to the hospital in the car I went through everything I had done that morning and how long it had taken me.

The doctor had said go home and I had.

And I missed it.

When we came to the sweeping bend down towards the town, the sense of urgency that had been lacking before now choked me.

'Nick, we need to sing,' it was an absolute. We had to. My voice was spluttering and only managed to get half of each word out before I sniffed it back in again. Nick kept it going.

'All things bright and beautiful, all creatures great and small...'

I couldn't believe I had missed it.

We arrived at the hospital and the nurse smiled and started to tell me she was sorry in a stiff voice and that they would soon be making the body ready. I fled past her to my sister who was bent over the bed; she was humming a tune through her fingers which were clasped around my Mum's hands.

All things bright and beautiful.

'I'm so sorry I wasn't here for you, Mummy.' I put one arm around my sister and placed my other hand on my Mum's forehead. 'Go and be free now. You're free now. Go and dance in the garden. Take his hand and just dance. That's all you have to do now, Mummy, you're free.'

I noticed the nurse at the bottom of the bed was picking up her notes, looking like she needed to do or say something. But she didn't. Out of the corner of my eye I watched as she discreetly left. I was pleased and continued my flow of words urging my Mum to leave fully and take her place in heaven. I was desperate for her to believe that she could go with no ties.

I was overwhelmed by the bravery of her dying.

A brave lady.

I sat with my sister and my Mum. We sat for a long time quiet and still. Sounds from life beyond were muffled and comforting.

'When did it happen?' I asked Nadia, hoping that she hadn't missed it either.

'About half an hour ago, just before nine.'

'How was it?' I wanted the moment etched in my mind. I wanted it clear and bright and vivid.

'Well, she started to breathe funny, you know, noisily.' We turned our chairs to face each other. 'I could tell she was struggling so I took her hand and just said, "I'm here for you, Mum, just give me your strength and let go. We'll be fine, just give me your strength." And then she didn't breathe in again.'

Nadia looked beautiful. She had the glow of someone who had just witnessed something awesome.

She had.

We took each other in our arms. 'I'm so glad it was you,' I whispered to her, 'I'm so glad you were here. You gave her a gift today, Nad.'

My biggest worry had been the thought of my Mum hanging on and hovering between life and death. When the doctor had said it could be two weeks I was shocked. Somewhere deep down I knew my Mum would defy them.

It hadn't even been twenty-four hours. I was pleased about that.

I am
Satisfied.
The circle is complete.

What is wrong with me?

'There is something wrong with me.' I was deep in thought and berating myself for feeling content. 'Who the fuck is pleased when their own precious mother lies dead in a morgue?'

I thought and thought. I remembered at school being so good and normal that I would hope and pray for some sort of defect.

Rosie got braces.

My teeth were straight.

Alexandria got glasses.

I had 20/20 vision.

Lucky Lucy got a stookie.

I had stupid, stupid strong bones that would not break even if I fell awkwardly or lay on them at an angle through the night.

I was so physically well constructed I couldn't stand it. I had even thought about getting the words 'distinguishing feature' tattooed on my thigh.

But now things had changed.
Now I was an orphan.
At only twenty-six years old.
They could take their wonky teeth, cross eyes and bendy bones and go spin.

I was an orphan.

Preparations

The six of us congregated in the kitchen.

We were in that blank space that your tongue searches for between your teeth after an injection at the dentist.

Nadia, Nick, Ben and I sat at the table, Archie was in his usual soporific state in his car seat on the ground and Granny June sat apart from us in the corner. She looked small and bewildered. I didn't even want to imagine her pain. I caught her eye and blew a kiss. She smiled sadly back. I left her to her thoughts and turned to the group.

We sat with diaries, notepads and address books trying to organise a funeral. We had to have it before the weekend. The thought of our precious Mum alone in a cold room for an entire weekend seemed terrible to us all.

Where to start? What to do?

We opened the Yellow pages and looked up Undertakers. The first one we tried might as well have been called 'Welcome to the Darkness funeral parlour'. It took an age for the phone to answer.

'Hello?' said a crackling faint voice which conjured images of a mothballed suit and candlesticks. I put down the phone before talking lest he cast a curse through the line and damned us to hell.

'Please tell me there's another undertaker.' I had no idea just what was involved in organising such an event. That's what it felt like. An event.

The Device, The Devil & Me

Ben found the number for the Smith Brothers in the local town. The Smith Brothers were twins and had come recommended by the minister. I felt a lump rise in my throat as I dialled the number. The answer was almost instant.

'Smith Brothers' funeral parlour. This is Andrew speaking. How may I help?' said a friendly voice.

I swallowed the lump. 'Oh hello, Mr Speaken, it's Lauren Walker here. My Mum has just died and I was wondering if you are available to do the service before the weekend.'

'Oh, I'm really sorry to hear that. I'm sure we will be able to accommodate you.'

I noticed Ben was stifling a giggle, the unmistakable quaking of the shoulders. What the hell could he possibly be laughing at now? I tried to ignore him and answer questions on embalming (no, she, we wouldn't want that) and coffins (plain) but everyone else's cheeks were reddening now. I gave them warning looks while I made the preliminary bookings for my mother's burial. The undertakers would be round in the morning to finalise everything.

'What was that all about?' I asked, completely puzzled and angry at the hilarity in the background. It wasn't them trying to hold it together on the phone to the last intimate contact to another human my Mum would have.

'Lauren, who were you talking to?' Ben smiled.

'One of the undertakers. Andrew.'

'What, you mean Andrew Smith, one of the Smith brothers?'

'Oh.' It started to dawn on me. 'So he's not called Mr Speaken then...' How that man didn't react I'll never know, but it was definitely an example of extreme professionalism.

When he arrived the next morning in his immaculate dark suit and immaculate concerned expression, I'm sure he didn't expect the smiling reception. We explained about the name. He was lovely and really put us at ease. It almost felt as though we were arranging a party.

They picked up 'the body' from the hospital and Nadia and I decided on which clothes she would wear to the other side. We chose her walking outfit, beige jumper, combats, full length Barbour jacket, clogs and hat. We also made sure the little empty strapless bra she'd worn was to be put on. We kept her jewellery to share amongst us as reminders, to keep her close.

My hands wrapped around the St Christopher I'd given to her for her hike in Namibia as Nadia fastened it behind my neck.

'It's really happened, hasn't it?' she said, putting my Mum's Thor necklace over her own head.

'Yes.' We looked at each other for a second then looked away before any evidence of tears appeared. We couldn't fall apart.

Not yet.

The funeral parlour was miserable in a trying-not-to-be-miserable-and-looking-exactly-like-what-is-expected kind of way. It was the complete lack of anything offensive that I found so offensive. The immaculate green carpeting, the beautifully dusted silk flower display, the wonderfully polished dark wood effect panelling and brochure laden coffee table. Even the piped organ music was exquisitely safe. Perfect hushed volume. It was so exactly what you would expect. I felt pity for the lovely Smith brothers and their perfect funeral parlour. Pity. It was one of the reasons I found myself so difficult to live with. Why did I pity people all the time?

Such conceit.

'It won't be a minute; we're just finishing with the other family.' One of the twins popped his head respectfully around the door. We nodded and smiled acceptance.

'What, there's only one room? You mean another dead person's just being wheeled out?' Nadia looked spooked. I had visions of the Smith brothers wheeling bodies in and out in rapid succession, whisking off a silk shawl and unveiling the open coffins with a magician's flourish.

'Da-dah!'

It was our turn.

For a small room it took ages to walk across. From the doorway, you could just see the face over the side of the wood. We urged each other on and held each other back, half shuffling, half striding. Stuck between fear and bravado.

When I eventually peered in, it wasn't that bad. I got a fright at how easy it was.

'Oo, hi Mum!' I said in a surprised way, as if I'd bumped into her unexpectedly in a shop or something. Nadia started forward as if she expected something. It reminded me of when my Grandfather died. I must have been about thirteen or something. It was the middle of the night when my Mum had answered the phone and sent us shivering to the car in whichever clothes we picked up first from the floor.

Granny June was sitting in the corner armchair bowed over with one of Grandpa's handkerchiefs clamped to her face. I have always got the fear when I hear Granny June cry. It comes from an unreal place like the back of her head and resonates in her soft palate with a grunt.

A doctor had arrived there before us and was tending to the body. My Mum had gone through to see her Dad and I had knelt on the floor in the living room rocking and rocking. I was crying. I couldn't believe my lovely jolly Grandpa was dead. I cried and whispered under my breath over and over, 'Don't be dead. Please don't be dead.'

After a while the doctor came through and put his hand on my shoulder and said soothingly, 'Come and see your grandfather, Lauren. It's all right – he's all right.'

Adrenalin coursed through my body and I jumped up and sprang through to the bedroom in excitement.

But when I got there he wasn't all right.

He was dead.

I hoped by speaking to my Mum in a familiar way that I hadn't stirred the same feelings in Nadia. I panicked and looked at her. She was smoothing my Mum's forehead, her face was crumpled with tears, but she was smiling.

It was a beautiful sight.

I put my arms around her.

Waving goodbye, saying hello

On the Thursday morning of the funeral, it felt like a party as my sister and I dressed in white suits and got into the big white limousine.

When the service was over, I stood in the dark entrance, my sister on my right, Nick on my left.

I shook the queue of hands with a smile on my face and thankyous on my lips. The people were dabbing their eyes and sniffing but I kept smiling.

I really actually did feel happy. Archie had made sure of it by sitting on the top of the pew in front where the hymn books perched and giggling the whole way through the service.

The coffin had looked tiny and precious but my baby had laughed and broken the spell of sadness that could have settled on us.

It had felt right.

The happiness had lifted me through and the handshaking was a good experience. There were people I knew well, people I hadn't seen for a while and people my Mum had known away and secret from me. Everyone introduced themselves whether they needed to or not. It was lovely to see them all.

I heard the warning come from my left just too late.

'He's here...' someone hissed just as I took the warm hand of a familiar man.

I recognised him instantly. The space around him darkened and expanded while he seemed to get smaller and paler and smaller.

'Oh, how good of you to come.'

'She was an amazing woman,' the voice quivered and his hands shook in a way I remembered so clearly. I held them fast and thanked him for showing up.

'Will you be at the reception?'

'If I'm allowed.'

'Of course, everyone is invited.'

'Thank you.'

I gave my father's hands an extra squeeze, hugged him and turned to the next hand while he moved along to my sister. I didn't see what happened between them but he was out of the church as I reached for the next person.

*

I managed to open my eyes not too long after I had woken up.

It was later than I thought and the baby was still asleep in his travel crib.

'Wow, he slept well.' I gave Nick a nudge that spread the ripples of a hangover through me. I decided not to lift my head off the pillow just yet.

'He was up three times. I didn't think you'd remember.'

I didn't remember.

I tried to think about what I did remember. Nothing after getting back from the reception. In fact, I couldn't even remember how we got home.

I could, however, remember the conversation my sister had with him.

My sister was drunk and aggressive. I think she's hilarious like that but her manner had got us in trouble before on girly nights out.

We were sitting in the remotest corner of the hotel bar with our estranged father. The hub and chatter sombrely waded around us, and the hundred pounds we had put behind the bar had been drunk already. I think someone had ordered champagne and my mind was wishing for a refill.

It could have gone so differently. It could have been a disaster. I was glad that an old familiar woman had come over to me and not my sister.

'Go and speak to your Dad, eh? It's hard for him too,' she said and I had felt rage flush through me and imagined scoring my fingernails through her weathered flesh. I managed to compose myself as I glanced to where he was sitting at a table of old people with old faces, his old friends. That was who she was. It was a shock: the woman standing in front of me used to be my aunt, all those years ago. She wasn't a real aunt, just a friend. The passage of time branded itself on my mind. It had been so quick and so long.

'Tell him I'm very sorry it's been hard on him. If he wants to speak to me he can come and get me.' I walked away stiffly half thinking he wouldn't come but I was surprisingly pleased when he did. I found us a quiet table and ushered my sister over.

As we sat together, I felt the familiar pity wash over me.

I was strong.
He was weak.
She was dead.

'I couldn't believe it when I read it in the paper.' He told us. 'When I saw the name it didn't register. It was the words after that that hit me.' My sister and I had been flamboyant in our wording of the announcements in the papers: 'Wonderful, loving mother and compositor extraordinaire' we had put as the tribute. Maybe we had subconsciously put it as a calling to him. He would never have been here had it not been for those two words: compositor and extraordinaire.

Even now with him sitting before me, it is easy.
   Even now with her dead, it is easy.
I am calm.
I am content.
I am unhurried.
I have space.

I had welcomed him and tried to make him feel at ease, but Nadia had grudges bubbling at the surface. She was drunk, falling down drunk, belligerent and witty.

'What the fuck are you doing here anyway, you twister?' Her eyes, yellowing with alcohol, held him in a cold stare.

'I've got every right to be here. This has been really hard for me, you know.'

Nadia nearly choked and spat a laugh of contempt at him.

'Poor you, David, poor, poor you.' She downed the rest of her double brandy and ginger.

'Don't you think you've had enough?'

'Fuck off. This was my Mum's drink and I will drink as much as I want. Who are you to tell ME what to do?'

'I am your father.'

'That's right, David. You ARE my father.' Her tone was becoming threatening through her drunken smiles. David looked to me as an ally, a way out of the very awkward situation, but suddenly, I felt empowered by Nadia's angry honesty.

'Oh no, David. You will listen to what this girl has to say,' I said, feeling brave. 'Think of it as looking into a mirror.' I watched in awe as my sister attacked our father with the words I myself longed to have the strength to wield. His counter attacks only fired her fury even more. As I observed the clash I felt myself pulling back and delving into the memories that had brought us to this point.

Shouting.

Him crying.

Pity.

Shaking.

Him crying.

Pity.

'If you don't mind,' I said and rose from my chair, grasping Nadia's angry shoulders. 'I need to check Archie and get this girl home.'

Thankfully, during the exchange between them, *thankfully*, he had not resorted to tears. I became aware that maybe this was reserved for me. Nadia reluctantly yielded to the pull on her shoulders and got up.

'Goodbye, David,' she smirked.

He ignored her.

'Em, bye then,' I said to him. I watched his eyes fill up and I wanted to run. I turned to Nadia but she was already at the bar.

'Wait,' he said, reaching out to catch my hand. I froze as he almost got it. 'Tell Nick I really appreciated him letting me hold Archie. He's beautiful.'

He held Archie? Nick had let him? I was pleased. I was glad he had held his grandson.

'He didn't need to do that. Tell him thank you.' I could see he was overwhelmed by Nick's act and so was I.

'He looks just like you, don't you think?' I said, smiling despite myself.

'Well, I wouldn't say that. But he is a wee stunner.'

I looked around the room.

'Okay, I'm going to go now. This has been, well, you know. . .'

I looked down.

'Lauren, will you promise me something?'

Oh God, not again. I braced myself.

'Will you drop me a line, even just a wee photo of him, from time to time?'

Guiltily, I prepared to make another promise to this man that I knew I would not keep. 'Sure, Daddy.' I walked away to my friends and drank several shots of whisky in quick succession.

'To Joyce!' we toasted.

I later sensed that he was gone but I hadn't seen him leave.

*

'You all right?' Nick gently clasped my hair and gave me a kiss, breaking me free from my thoughts. 'You were in some state last night.'

'Nick!' I was suddenly defensive. 'Fuck's sake, I think I had a right to be.'

'I know, I know, darling,' he soothed. 'I'm not giving you a row.'

I rolled over to face him. 'I know, sorry.' I had an image making its way into my visual imagination that I wasn't quite sure I wanted to see. 'Nick. . . ?'

'Yes?'

'If the baby was up three times last night, how on earth did you get him back to sleep?' Nick looked at me, eyebrows raised.

'I had to, you know, lift up your nightie and stick him on!'

'But I didn't even notice!' The image that had been forming was now in plain view. I brought my hand up to my mouth to cover my smile. 'Bloody hell, Nick, I was in some state last night, eh?'

Rules rules rules

I like rules.
   I like good rules.
   I like keeping the good rules.
   The ones that make sense.
   I can't, however, keep silly rules.
   Like...
   Put the cold in first.
   NO.
   Or
   Shave in the direction of the hair growth.
   NO.

The Creeping

The dark sea so gently laps at the sand.
A stirring. A ripple.
There, I'm sure I saw it.
There it is again.
There's something underneath pressing
the surface.
The water will not yield. It keeps it
held. It looks like a hand.
It's my mother's hand.
Cold and dead.

'It hasn't worked.' Her eyes are the colour of
blood and that hand reaches out.
'Tell them it hasn't worked... Tell them I'm still alive.'
I scramble backwards in my visitor's chair in
terror and search for a doctor.
But my chair is not there.
It's just sand.
Just sand and sea.
Reaching out for ever.
There it is again, that ripple is different.
It's colder.
It wants to break and show me its secrets.
I know it will only be there in the dead of night.
Like glass shattering.
Why are you still here?
Nick said you come to visit him. Sometimes it's fleeting.
Sometimes you stay for a chat.
I don't ask him what you talk about.
I don't want to know.
I don't want to know because I know it will be
only nice and good things.
You will smile.
You won't stare out at him through wild bloodshot eyes
and ask him why you are still here.
Your stiff bones won't crack as you reach out to him.
No.
I don't want to know.
The ripples retreat for now.
Waiting.

Aftermath

The serenity continued. I lived in a mist of breastfeeding and love. Motherhood fulfilled me.

Archie had smiled and gurgled me happy. I picked up the phone to tell my Mum he had rolled over for the first time. As I dialled the number and my sister answered I remembered.

'Oh hiya!' I said, trying not to sound crushed. 'Archie rolled over.' We ooed and ahhed together and I managed to convince myself that she was the one I had wanted to tell all along.

It was the catching yourself that was the strangest thing. Like stepping down stairs when you think there's another step to go. The jolt is unbelievable. How can your foot be so heavy?

The ground so hard?

The contact so definite?

We chatted and put the phone down. I felt empty. The happy comfortable space I was now used to was gone; in its place was a dull emptiness. I looked at my baby, now an expert at flipping over and over. He was nearly out of the door. I retrieved him and felt the void filling again.

'Come on, sweetpea, let's try a bottle, shall we?' I had been trying to wean him on to the bottle since the funeral. He just was not interested and I was feeling worn out. Breastfeeding, though magical and perfect, was beginning to take its toll on me. It was exhausting, I was constantly hungry and felt my flabby cumbersome body was nothing like the one I should have. It didn't help that Victoria Beckham had popped out a child at the same time as me and well, let's just leave it at that, shall we?

I warmed the sterilised bottle of powder and water and pushed it to my baby's lips. He dramatically and defiantly twisted his head from side to side like an eel on a line.

I tried everything: pushing the rubber nipple in his mouth alongside mine, trying to catch him unawares while he was asleep, coating the teat with breast milk. He would not give in. He would scream and scream until I popped one of my massive boobs into his face. It started to frustrate me.

'Come on, darling, Mummy needs a wee break,' I said softly. It had been four weeks of trying; I'd even left him in the house, starving, with Nick so that his only option would be to take it. Four hours of screaming later I had arrived home to a wild-eyed Nick who passed me the baby before I was even through the front door.

I was so tired.

I took us both through to the sofa and lifted my jumper. I scrunched up my eyes and began to cry.

When he was full and sleeping I carried him through and placed him in his crib. He was so beautiful.

I went to the bathroom and looked at my face.

It was red and fat and tired and old. Badness bubbled in me and something welled in the pit of my stomach. I grabbed my hair at the temples and spat at my own horrible reflection.

NO, no, no.
My lovely space has developed a shadow.
I check and recheck, holding my breath.
Yes, there it is, just there.

I catch it in my peripheral vision for a second.
But it's enough.
It's there.

I rocked and rocked the little crib pleading with every pore of my body for the little soul to go to sleep.

I sang and smiled and cooed but my heart was beating wild and fast. I was just desperate to sit in a place on my own, on my sofa, by myself and smoke.

The baby finally let out a sigh and closed his eyes. I almost ran through to the living room which was all prepared. The window was open, remote controls near to hand and ashtray, cigarette and lighter lay waiting for my touch. I lifted the joint to my lips and inhaled deeply. I held the smoke in and let my guilt build.

Relief. My muscles relaxed and I flopped my head back into the sofa.

Shit, had I locked the front door? I put down the ashtray and padded through to check.

Of course I had locked it.

I swept back through and jumped onto the cushions with the same breath still jammed in my lungs.

Exhale.

Relax.

It's just paranoia.

I stand at the edge

It was time to go back to work.

The baby was safe and happy with his tiny peers in a little private nursery.

I had just left him, then driven up Arthur's Seat, and parked at the top car park. I was so disappointed. I thought I had won my battle. I thought it was over. But as I sat in my car with cigarette papers littering my lap I knew I was in trouble.

I was angry, frustrated, despondent.

I looked at the view, at the swans and signets, at bread being thrown to hungry ducks, at mothers and prams and I felt nothing.

'Let's go feed the ducks,' Nick would sometimes say.

'I hate feeding the ducks, Nick.'

'Everyone likes feeding the ducks.'

I would get angry. 'Well, not everyone, Nick.'

As a little girl on a Saturday afternoon, I would sit at the window with my heart in my throat waiting for my Dad to pick up me and my sister. He would arrive late then take us to feed the ducks with a bag of stale bread, muttering about being a baby sitter and my Mum using him.

I knew even then that his bitterness was astounding. He grudged taking his own daughters out for four hours once a week in case it gave my Mum the freedom to do something for herself. Nor was I naïve enough not to know why he always came late and dropped us off early.

He wanted to catch her out.

So now I hate feeding the fucking ducks.

Not only that, I hate watching people feeding the fucking ducks. But on that day, sitting in my car, without my baby, I wallowed in my hatred for it.

I rolled my joint as the bread flew into open squawking mouths.

'Better to have loved and lost than never to have loved,' my Mum used to say. I would always agree with her but now, standing at the edge of this precipice, I wasn't so sure. I had tasted freedom from my demons and it had been so delicious, so sweet that the thought of going back to where I was before was more than I could bear. It had been easier to live with then. Before I had known any better. Now though, I knew what normal was because for a short while, I had lived it.

I couldn't go back, I couldn't.

I lit my joint and took a few steps closer.

I inhaled.

> *The truth.*
> *Are you flirting with me?*
> *What?*
> *Did I answer?*
> *Rule no.1: NEVER engage in any form of communication.*
> *I said, are you flirting with me?*
> *His voice is velvet, I can taste it.*
> *I clap my hands to my face.*
> *Well, are you?*
> *How could I have been so stupid?*

Why do you ask? I only thought it.
I only thought it.
He laughs.
He heard.
Of course I heard.
It has happened.
He is back in.

I opened the shop. It was like I had never been away.

I took out the sign and put the kettle on. It felt as though I had been away for years.

Charles had manned the bookstore himself for the six months I was away on my maternity leave. It had felt like whole life leave, not just maternity leave. He had left me lilies, chocolates and champagne on the counter as welcome back presents. They had an air of desperation about them... as if he was saying, 'Thank God you're back! I can get to the golf course now!' The fact that he wasn't here in person confirmed my suspicions. He felt like he'd done his time serving customers and the state of the place was testament to that. I had a busy day ahead and it made me smile to think of distracted old Charles wafting about the place in his smoking jacket. I hoped he'd pop in soon.

I eyed the chocolates and felt my mouth water. I opened the box and took it through to the kitchen. I turned on the hot tap and let it run until it was scalding then held the chocolates under it. When they were suitably spoiled, I tipped them into the bin and closed the lid.

I put the lilies into the best glass vase I could find and put them in the window.

I put the champagne in my bag.

With good intentions of dealing with six months of neglect, I took out the cleaning box then spent the day doodling on the sales book and pining for Archie.

If you wanted me to go, you only needed to tell me.

But you didn't.

You want me here.

You want me.

I feel my energy being pulled and stretched out to the corners of the room leaving me tired and limp in the middle. I am held on a sheet of my own exhaustion ready to be bounced up and down like the birthday bumps.

I am so weak.

He is right.

I want Him.

If I didn't I would tell.

He's right.

You told about the pathetic eating thing.

Now that's gone.

You told about the cutting.

Now that's gone.

Shame.

I liked it.

But you haven't told anyone about me.

Have you?

That's why I'm still here.

You want me.

I don't tell anyone about you because no one would believe me.

I would be locked up.
Rule no.2: NEVER explain yourself.
The other things were easy.
Easy to give up.
His words tickle the nape of my neck and creep down my shoulder.
I breathe out.

A cosy chat

I found myself back at the Maggie's Centre.

I still felt that I had no right to be there but somehow my body had pulled me back there.

I looked at the kitchen area where, as a cancer patient's relative, I was welcome to make myself a cup of tea.

I checked myself.

I wasn't a cancer patient's relative.

I was a cancer victim's relative.

There was a big difference. Was I still allowed in?

I was desperate to be welcomed into the fold.

I didn't want a cup of tea. I hung around the pamphlet and book rack and picked one up. And put it back.

I waited and hoped someone would come and talk to me. Eventually I moved over to a typing man who looked thoroughly engrossed in his task. It was Gary, the co-ordinator of the Namibian hike.

'Hi, it's Lauren, Joyce's daughter, Joyce from the hike.'

'Oh yeah, Joyce,' he was very warm and smiled kindly. 'How is she?'

'She's dead.'

He told me how sorry he was and pulled a chair out for me. We sat opposite each other with Archie asleep in his car seat on the floor next to my left foot.

'How are you coping?'

I let it out.

'I feel like knives are raining down on me and I want them to pierce my skin.'

He looked shocked then concerned. I looked down at Archie.

'You light up when you look at your baby.'

'Oh, he's my absolute pride and joy. That's what makes me feel even more guilty. Why am I feeling like this when I have an angel by my side?'

'I think you should go to your doctor.'

Shit.

Not again.

And me.
I could just lie back.
I could just give in.
And. . .
Lie. . .
Back.
It would be so easy.
It would be so. . .
His breath raises a trail of tiny hairs wherever it goes. It snakes to my arms, around to my breast bone and hovers. . .
And waits. . .
For surrender.
I breathe in.
The battle could be so over quickly.
I feel an arousal. The relief is tangible. I am on the edge of a cliff so high.
I have never been this close to the abyss.

*I have never felt so relaxed, at peace and not unafraid.
I like this feeling.
It would only take one step.
Like a film, my toe disturbs some gravel and I watch it fall silently down into the darkness of his arms.*

The Cure: Part 1

So far I had filled in my name, age and date of birth. There wasn't much to it. The form lay on my lap clipped to one of those plastic-clad clipboards, the kind that you want to make holes in with your teeth and peel back to look at the dents where other pens have pressed through.

There was one question left.

'Why have you come here today?'

I thought about my answer. I thought about writing: 'Because that's when the appointment was made.' I couldn't think of any part of my body that hurt, I was just looking forward to a massage. I couldn't think of a physical problem to write in the box.

I had been given an alternative therapy voucher for my birthday and it had been in my bag for six weeks. By the time I finally got round to checking whether it was still valid I think I was secretly hoping it wasn't. The therapy centre helped consolidate this thought. It was dark and woodchipped with low brown ceilings, but it did have many certificates of excellence up on the stained walls. A small scruffy man with tufty hair had addressed me as 'my love' and told me to take a seat. Then he had handed me the questionnaire.

Before I knew it I had scribbled: 'Because I want to stab myself and I don't want to any more.' A battle raged between my mind and my pencil as I tried to score the words out. The lead hovered a fraction of a millimetre over the page as my hand made a frantic scribbling motion.

'Let's see...' George took the file and scanned it. I saw his eyes stop and I wished I had just gone ahead and scored it out. He looked me up and down and motioned me through to the treatment room.

I lay on my back and held up my arm as George had told me to.

He applied pressure with his fingers to points all over my body and as he did so he pushed my arm with his other hand.

'Just relax, lovely lady. I'm going to fix you.'

I believed him.

I didn't look into the corner where I knew He would be laughing and watching.

Place by place George moved his hands across my body: my collar bone, my chest, my belly, my pubis, and all the while he spoke numbers to a uniformed lady behind him. She was recording them on a chart and all I had to do was to keep my arm in the air. I started to hold my breath as the numbers increased.

'Relax, keep breathing.'

What if he gets to 666? There'll be no escape.

Something was happening.

I could feel something start to flow.

It was exactly what I wanted. I wanted to be told to lie down, shut my eyes and hand myself over.

'I'll fix you,' he had said.

And I had believed him.

My voucher had been for forty-five minutes of massage but when I looked at the clock as I floated out of the therapy room, I saw that he had given me over two hours. I knew that something magic had taken place.

'It's all about love, my beautiful lady,' the practitioner had said when I asked if I owed extra for his time. He hugged me to him tight and long and I caught my breath as I thought he was going to kiss me full on the lips but he stopped at my cheek.

'Can I come back?'

'You must.'

I made an appointment for the next week and hovered back to my car. Gravity had eased its grip on my ankles.

Something had lifted.

I wanted to keep it that way.

I parked the car outside my house and just sat for a while.

I really did feel different. I looked at my reflection in the rearview mirror and smiled. It was a smile that came from deep within me, further in than I had ever known. Even when I had been well with motherhood there was a certain cautiousness. I looked again, straight into my own eyes without fear. My gaze didn't waver as I explored the person whom I knew intimately and not at all.

I thought of my Mum almost wearing out the glass in her rearview applying lipstick to pouting lips. I raked around in the glove compartment until I found half a lipstick without a lid. After I had picked off the bits of grit and dirt with my fingernails I pulled the greasy stick over my mouth. I looked alien yet comfortable. I turned my head this way and that, grinning with teeth, smiling without, laughing openmouthed. I pulled my lower eyelids down and checked for anaemia.

Yup, looked pretty anaemic to me. Though any blood tests had always shown perfect haemoglobin levels. Finally, after smoothing down my hair, I left the car and stood at my front door.

I felt new.

When Nick looked up at me from the TV he paused, then jumped up.

'My, you look different.'

I shyly touched my lips.

'No, it's not that, come here and kiss me.' He drew me to him.

> *Don't get too excited.*
> *What?*
> *Who said that?*

Later in bed, trying to get comfy after my extreme high had subsided, I couldn't shake off a nagging feeling that I had had – if I were honest – since the appointment with George.

Had he been flirting with me? Was my ego just getting me into trouble? Was I exchanging one Devil for another?

No, he was good.

He was kind.

He was...

I remembered his warm hands languidly taking their time over my body as I had lain stiff as a board, trying to force my lungs still.

I remembered his arms around me just before I had left embracing me and me embracing him back so as not to appear rude.

But surely none of that mattered? He was curing me. I could feel it!

I decided that I was probably just trying to sabotage my own healing process and pulled the covers over me.

At work for the next few days I was calm and level and happy. I was relaxed.

It was only towards the end of the week when my appointment drew nearer that I began to get slightly jumpy.

Maybe I wouldn't need to go again.

Maybe that was enough already. I was feeling great. I really was, wasn't I?

Everything had gone so smoothly all week.

The morning of the appointment I took a delivery of three huge boxes of books. As I took them through to the back room for pricing and sorting, I tripped on a corner of rug and hit my head on the doorway. The blackness surrounded me so quickly and with such rage that I had to smack my knuckles into the wall over and over until I could smell blood.

I stopped shocked and exhausted.

I heard a customer come into the shop and shouted, 'I'll just be a second' and ran my hands under cold water.

I was shaking. What the fuck had just happened? I wanted to cry and cry but I managed to pull myself together. That was one of the worst rages I had had since before I was pregnant. I just couldn't believe how quickly it had come over me and how totally I had given in to it.

I wrapped my still bleeding hand in toilet paper and took my place behind the counter.

I felt like a danger.

I would definitely keep my appointment.

The Cure: Part 2

I sat in the scruffy bathroom which looked like it could do with a scrub. Lord knows I am not on terribly familiar terms with any sort of cleaning product but this was a million miles away from the pristine white palaces my Mum used to take me to for waxings and facials.

It was definitely a man's bathroom.

Nothing quite matched and the grouting between the tiles was black. I felt the same crawling anticipation I had last time and had to keep reminding myself of how good I had felt afterwards.

I went through to the treatment room.

'Hello, my darling. I'll leave you to get comfortable.'

The dingy room. The familiar beige woodchip on the walls. There were no bleached white sheets on the table, only an old floral duvet cover.

I took off my shoes and climbed onto the table fully clothed and covered myself with the green towel provided.

I lay and lay, breathing shallowly while I studied my unlikely surroundings.

A knock.

'Are you ready, my love?' he asked as he came through the door. 'I think we'll do something different today. Why don't you take off your top half?'

'Okay,' I said, as I sat up and waited for him to leave the room again.

'Don't worry, I'm here to help you.'

I started taking my jumper off and then my t-shirt. I sat with my bra on with him behind me. My breathing quickened again and I felt bewildered.

Ha ha! You can't trust him.
You idiot.
You think a bearded man with a framed paper certificate on his walls can get rid of Me?
He's not even going to try.

'Look, stop being nervous. You are a beautiful lady. I'm never going to hurt you. Come on, take off your bra.'

I held my breath and lay face down on the table naked from the waist up, all the while feeling his eyes watching and stroking me. He attached two heavy electrodes to me – one at the top left shoulder and one at the right hip, then turned on a loud machine. Vibrations rang through my body. I tried to let go and relax my muscles and allow the current to pass through.

'I'm just going to leave you for a while.' And away he went.

I felt cheated. I wanted human hands not machinery. I concentrated on not hearing that voice.

Ten minutes passed, then twenty.

My muscles were relaxing but my mind was tensing.

Just in time, he came back and switched off the machine, removed the electrodes, put a towel over me and asked me to turn over.

His hands were strong as they pressed into my skull. It was like all I ever needed was happening now. The harder he massaged and the further he moved, the closer I felt to myself. I was letting go.

I felt safe.

But then he was talking. Telling me to relax. Telling me to relax as he began to count backwards...

Ten... I stiffened

Nine... I closed my ears

Eight... I let my heart race

Seven... I pulled out my lead barriers and quickly assembled them tight around my head

Six... Get away. I threw the words at him silently. You're not getting in.

Five... I was alert

Four... I was on high alert

Three... Do not come in here, I raged

Two... My body seared with tension

One... I checked myself

Good. I was still conscious. I was still awake.

It hadn't worked.

As the session drew to a close I asked, 'You tried to hypnotise me, didn't you?'

'You wouldn't let me, my darling.'

I was pleased. He had really tried and I had repelled him.

I did have power.

Once again I left the clinic feeling light and happy.

You've got to fight. . .

I had been feeling so good that Nick and I decided to hold a summer party. I am always more content and at ease when I have something to organise. A task to fulfil. I checked the dates and phoned everyone I could think of. I was really excited and managed to finish the last few invitations before my appointment.

The tension that usually shrouded me as I entered George's clinic was delightfully absent.

'Well, my, my. Look at you, my love.' He stood before me holding both my hands and gazing straight into my eyes. He leaned in. 'It's working, isn't it?'

I allowed myself to beam back.

'Yes, yes! I can feel it. I am even organising a party to celebrate!'

'That's great, my love.' He let go of my hands and turned me with a palm on my shoulder and ushered me through. 'Let's get this finished, Cinderella.'

> *You're making a mistake.*
> *You'll never survive without me.*
> *I smile.*
> *I can, I will.*
> *You are only a whisper now.*

George worked my shoulders, my back, my thighs, my calves, my feet.

Ahhhhh…It felt so good. I felt so relaxed.

'Are you feeling good, my love?'

'Mmmmm,' I nodded my head into the pillow.

'Okay, sweet lady, roll over.' So I rolled under cover of a green towel and replaced my head easily back into position.

'We'll try something a bit different today,' he said as he clutched the base of my skull in both hands. I let myself melt. He was quiet. I was pleased.

Then he spoke.

'You need to let your mother go.'

The spell was broken. The damn gates smashed and tension crashed through.

'I have let her go, she's dead.' My voice was cold. 'I told her to go and dance in the garden, for God's sake.'

'How can she dance when you have her skirts so tightly wrapped around you?'

Ha ha!
Ha.
You are done.

Something stirred in the shadows of the room.

He was wrong. I had told her to go. I *had* let her go. I told her to be free! Why was he saying this?

His fingers ground into my scalp trying to soothe me but it felt like there was no flesh between us. The bare bones of his fingers scraped over the wet bone of my head. The casing of my doom. He was looking for a lock to pick.

He found it.

I felt cooling tears trickle into my ears, making me shiver. I reached up to wipe them but he stopped me and gently placed my arms back against my side. He continued on the way up, pressing my body gently and firmly with his palms towards my head.

'Let them out. You're safe.'

I did. I was.

*

I see, I dream

I see you. You look down at me, pitifully
kneeling at your feet.
Clutching.
Gripping.
Your face is full of wretched concern but your eyes
keep flicking desperately skyward.
I look down at my hands, folds and folds of fabric
encase them winding tighter and tighter.
I feel horror as if they are covered in blood.
I have you anchored to me.
I am so sorry.
Your kind eyes soften and the worry starts to fade.
I am so sorry.
I slowly unbind myself, carefully unwrapping. Like the
first tentative removal of bandages after an amputation.
What will be left?
I feel you gently tug. You are like a kite
on a soft breeze.

> As my small white hands are revealed, you are high
> above me. Your face is alight with peace.
> The last threads slide between my fingers and I look up
> at you as they slip away.
> You are gone.

*

My hair was soaked with tears and George rubbed them into my head. Restoring them back into my pores.

I lay in silence and exhaustion for the next half hour at his mercy.

When we walked quietly through to the reception desk, he hugged me once again.

I handed him his money and nodded to him through lowered lids.

'Thank you,' he nodded back. I left.

For your right...

Dipping my hands into the warm, sticky red mixture felt divine. It oozed through my fingers as I smoothed it over slippery paper strips.

I was applying the finishing layer of papier-mâché to my piñata for the party. I had made the paste by heating up flour and water and I had poured in a bottle of red food colouring. I could have just painted it at the end but I wanted it to be the colour of blood from the inside out. It had taken me a week to build up enough layers to make it self supporting. Six thick layers sat beneath my hands. By day I had worked in the shop with stained fingers and by night I had created.

At last, the huge balloon I had blown to its maximum strain had been covered and strengthened. I laid it wet one last time next to the radiator.

'You don't think you're overdoing it, do you, darling? You're working awfully hard for a get together.' Nick came in and rolled his eyes at my creation.

'It's not a get together, Nick, it's a party. And no, you can't work too hard to make a party.' I was angry that his enthusiasm didn't match mine. I didn't even know if he'd asked his friends yet.

I stopped what I was doing and wiped my hands. I stood before him and looked into his face.

'Please darling, this means a lot to me. Please let me do it.' I had been buying, making, finding decorations, stocking up on booze, cooking food and freezing it.

'I know, I know. I just don't want you to exhaust yourself. What if, you know, it's a disaster and no one comes.'

'Nick,' I could see he was genuinely concerned. I had been on quite a high doing all the organising and I could tell he thought I was becoming manic. 'It won't be a disaster. If nobody comes, it doesn't matter. You'll be there. I'll be there. Just let me do this.' I held his hands and pleaded with my eyes. Please be enthusiastic for me, I silently implored.

'All right, darling,' he said, ruffling my hair. 'Come on let's get decorating.'

The only job left for that evening was to tidy up the mess I had made. As I picked up strands of torn paper and scooped leftover glue into the bin and washed the brushes and pans, Nick began to fold up the, as yet, unread sports section, then started to read it. I smiled and continued my cleaning.

*

I made my way along the street to my last appointment with George before my party. I was actually looking forward to this session. I couldn't think of any other stones that were left for him to rake under so I was anticipating a nice relaxing deep tissue massage.

I felt taller and lighter as I breezed through to the treatment room. George was having coffee with another practitioner and they smiled when they saw me.

'See,' he motioned to the other man, 'I told you, unrecognisable isn't she?' I smiled and the colleague nodded back before shuffling out of the room, coffee and biscuits in hand.

I readied myself and lay down on the now familiar and homely bed. It was really a treatment table but it felt like a bed.

'So, let's see...' George ran his hand down my spine to my heels, 'what are we looking for today?'

'Well, it's my party this weekend so I think I would like a relaxing yet invigorating deep tissue massage please.'

'Oh yes, your party. You must let me know where you live so I can find it.'

What? No! I didn't... I wouldn't. I... The excitement evaporated. I didn't want him to come. Why had he asked? Why had I been so stupid and mentioned it in the first place? I felt sorry for him.

I was thrown back in time...

I am ten. I am in a five-a-side football tournament in the next village from ours. I have been so excited about this all week, training, getting my strip together. This is just a t-shirt and shorts of any colour, the only unifying item being day-glo socks. We have swapped with one another so that no one has a matching pair. We watch the other teams get off their buses with their professional kits adorned with local sponsorship logos. Then I remember. I haven't phoned him! I haven't called him all week. Oh no, he will be angry or sad. I run away from my team over the field and up to the public phone box behind the café. I don't have any money. Oh no, oh no, oh no... I reverse the charges. I listen to the lady's voice as the phone rings and rings at the other end.

'There's no answer, would you like me to try again?'

I am so relieved. 'No, thank you.' I run back to the pitch just as our first game is starting. It's only ten minutes each half and

I score a goal! We are in the lead. It is half-time and we all run to the woman with the oranges. I stop in my tracks.

A man comes towards me.

It is him.

'Hello, Daddy,' I say, trembling in my loomies, 'why are you here?'

'Because I wasn't invited,' he replies, his eyes wild.

'I tried to call you but there was no answer.' I am scared and guilty.

'No, you didn't, Lauren. I have been in all week and my phone hasn't rung once.'

What can I say? I don't know what to say. I don't know what to do. Bodies rush past me and the whistle goes for the second half. I keep my eyes down and follow them. I swap with Georgina and spend the next half standing still in goal.

'Why so tense, my love?' George's voice shocked me back into the treatment room.

'Don't know, guess I need a massage.'

Stupid fucking party.

I didn't want it now.

He peeled back the towel and once again placed his warm hands on my back. I made a decision to put everything out of my mind. I didn't want to spoil my time any more. I eased myself down into the mattress and let it hold my full weight. My head sank down and stopped, suspended yet held. I breathed with his movements and slowly managed to rid myself of the scene I had replayed.

He was going slowly and thoroughly, not missing a knot. It

was heaven. When he had covered every millimetre of my back and legs he asked me to turn over.

I did so and let my head fall into his cradling hands. He held me like that for a while, slowly pressing with his finger tips in a pulsing motion.

'Lauren, my beauty?'

'Mmm, hmm?'

'You need to forgive your father.'

'What?' I sat straight up and turned to face him. 'What?' I couldn't find any other words. What was this man?

'None of this will be over for you until you do.'

He didn't know what he was talking about.

'You are angry with him and you need to forgive him and let that anger go.'

'I'm not angry.'

'Just forgive him. You will feel better.'

'I don't want to.'

'Then you will never be well.' George's face had a look of such sadness that I started to cry.

'I'm scared.' He supported me while I lay down again and cradled my head. He hummed a soft tune as he waited for me to still myself.

'Don't be afraid, beautiful one. I am here, I am here.'

So am I.

I reached into the depths of myself to find the calm. Part of me felt like a complete wally, lying in a pit of mumbo jumbo. Part of me didn't want to ridicule it. On this occasion I chose the latter. I listened to his voice.

'I want you to see yourself. I want you to look down at the ball and chain you have around your ankle.'

*

I see, I dream

'Now, if you want it to be gone. All you have to do is look at your Dad, go on, see him.'
I do.
'Now say, "I forgive you, Dad."'
I can't.
'Go on.'
Does he mean out loud? God, I can't bear it.
'He's never said sorry,' I stall.
'You don't know that,' George's voice is so solid and sure I believe that he believes. At this moment that is enough for me.
I visualise my Dad. I see him. He's laughing at a joke, he's making my wings, he's wound up, he's taking me fishing, he's shouting at my Mum, he's flying a kite, he's happy, he's vicious and spitting, he's sad and crying, he's angry, his car has broken down, he's pitiful, he stands before me.
He's sorry.
'I forgive you,' I say meekly in my own mind.
'Now say it out loud.'
'I can't.'
'You can.'
I do.

'I forgive you, Daddy.' He looks down and retreats into the shadows. I am crying and crying as the chains around my ankles soften and melt apart.

*

George told me to rest and lie a while to gather my thoughts. I watched him leave then lay listening to my heart racing. I felt as if I had run a million miles. I felt bewildered. I felt awkward and bare. I grabbed my clothes and dressed quickly and hastily.

I was dizzy.

I made my way through.

'See, you shall go to the ball, Cinderella.'

I paid George and left before he could ask me where I lived.

To Party

I waited, nervous and excited, for the guests to arrive.

We had managed to get Archie shipped out to a friend's for the night and I had a glass of sparkling wine which had been filled twice already. I gulped down a few more mouthfuls and checked myself again in the mirror.

I had dyed my hair, eyebrows and eyelashes black to match my black tights and new skirt. It was short and when I had tried it on in the shop I was startled at how good it looked.

'I have legs!' I thought with joy. It had been one of those rare and highly sought after trips to TK Maxx where everything I picked not only fitted me perfectly in size 12 but also looked great. I had a choice of about three different outfits. I chose, to my surprise, the very short black skirt with a high-necked red top. I pulled my tummy in and looked at myself from side to side.

I looked good.

I felt good.

I had paid for my clothes and gone home to a wonderful afternoon of dyeing, bathing, shaving, plucking, hoovering, catering and decorating and now it was time to get drunk.

Nick returned from dropping off the baby and joined me in a glass of fizz.

'Wow, you look fit for a party.'

I grinned. The doorbell rang.

By nine o'clock everyone we'd been expecting was drinking,

chatting and dancing. I felt invincible. Buoyed up by an intoxicating mixture of booze, friends and my newfound tranquillity and self-love, I was having the most amazing time.

'Could everyone gather in the living room please?' I rang my glass with a spoon and scurried through to the bedroom.

My piñata sat on my bed under a red tablecloth I had bought especially for this task. I picked it up by its suspension thread and carried it through. Everyone stood with their drinks in their hands, chatting and mingling.

It wasn't until I was standing on a chair in the middle of the room that they began to take notice.

'What are you up to?' my sister asked and came over to help. She lifted the hem of the tablecloth and I batted her hand away.

'No peeking!' I lifted the piñata higher and tried to reach the pendant light fixture. I hadn't checked if it was strong enough but had thought, Fuckit, it'll make it more exciting anyway. I strained to reach up as my guests became my audience, until at last Nick came to my rescue and took the rope from my hands. I jumped down and the air caught my skirt. I didn't care; I had bought new pants too.

Finally when Nick had tied up the strange red mass, I announced the game.

'Right, everyone, we all know that no party is complete without...' I held the corner of the cloth and with a flourish whisked it off, 'a piñata!'

At first there was silence as everyone took in the enormous blood red Devil which stared at them through menacing black and yellow eyes. I started to panic at the lack of response until Kitty declared, 'Fucking hell, Laur, that's amazing!'

Everyone started clapping and I did a little curtsy. The Devil's horns suspended above me glinted and I rejoiced that it, that He, was about to meet his doom.

I picked up the stick hidden behind the sofa along with the black and red velvet eye mask.

'Okay,' I grinned from ear to hear, 'who wants to go first?'

There was hesitation so I stepped up to Nick and handed him the stick. 'I think you should be the first.'

He struck the beast as hard as he could three times but didn't make a dent. I took the stick from him to background cheering and booing and passed it to Nadia.

'Come on, kill it!' She tried her best while our friends urged her on but did no better. Kitty was next.

'Go, go, go, go!' we all chanted. It was becoming obvious, as one by one we barely scratched the demon, that I had chosen the wrong weapon. The Devil stared at us, unmoved by our efforts.

Finally, after everyone had had a shot, I took the stick and stepped up to the piñata.

'Well now, Devil,' I declared dramatically, 'it's just you and me now.'

I lifted the stick like a Thundercat and cried, 'Sword of Omens, give me sight beyond sight!' I swung the stick back and just as I was about to batter the beast, someone grabbed my arm.

'Oi!' I turned to see Nick with a baseball bat in his hands.

'I think you need a new stick, m'lady.' I took the baseball bat and held it high. My friends laughed and I brought it down onto the hanging demon as hard as I could.

It cracked.

I swung again and it split. The insides became visible; treats could be seen through the tear.

I took one almighty swing and watched as the Devil smashed to pieces, sending white streamers, glitter and balloons all over the carpet and partygoers.

I was panting.

I was exhilarated.

'Sweets!' someone shouted and everyone started scrambling about on the floor, laughing and grappling for cola bottles and skull crushers.

Nick, Kitty and Nadia sought me out. They crowded me in a hug.

'Thank you.' I started to sniff, 'I. . .'

'Oh shut up,' Kitty cuffed me, 'let's fucking party!'

I wake up

It has been a day.

It has been a week.

It has been a month.

I feel myself awaken under my sleeping eyes. My heart skips a beat as I hold my breath and listen to my thoughts.

They are soft and calm.

My chest inflates gently as I breathe in.

It is a subtle change.

It is a huge change.

I peek around the corners of my mind with the covers pulled up to my chin.

Nothing.

I emerge from my nest and place my feet on the floor. They sink into the carpet but remain light.

I twist and look at my sleeping Nick. A strip of sunlight sears his face and his eyes twitch to avoid it. His breathing is quiet and long. He is so peaceful and I kiss his full warm lips lightly.

I stand up and cautiously pad through to the kitchen looking in on my sleeping baby on the way.

He is calm.

I am calm.

I put on the coffee and look out at the sunny day.

I switch on the radio. The unforgettable first lines. . .

'First I was afraid, I was petrified.'

My heart kicks in, bubbling with excitement.
'Kept thinking I could never live without you by my side.'
I could burst with the glorious realisation.
He is gone
I am free
He is gone
And I am me!
I jump and mosh and whoop and skip.
I am a lucky girl
I can dance.

FIN